WOBBLY TRUTHS

& Other Stories

by Natalie Scott

By the same author:

Novels

Wherever We Step the Land is Mined
Jonathan Cape, London & Franklin Watts, New York
The Glasshouse
Rigby, Adelaide

Short Stories

Eating Out & other stories
Winner of National Library TDK Audio Book Award, 1997, and
Society of Woman Writers Bi-annual Fiction Award, 1997
Eating Out Again & other stories
Otford Press, Sydney, Kuala Lumpur and Dili

For children

Firebrand
Wings on Wednesday
Hullabaloo
Please Sit Still
The Wizard of the Umbrella People

WOBBLY TRUTHS

& Other Stories

by Natalie Scott

978-0-6450566-2-4 (paperback)
978-0-6450566-3-1 (eBook)

Published by Bouley Bay Books, Sydney & Jersey
Tel: (+61) 403 039 164 Email: MLM444@gmail.com
Typeset & printed in Australia by Image DTO
Tel: 0423 360 883
Cover Design by Image DTO
Front cover image by Mems Mosaics

First published 2021
© Natalie Scott (2021)

For Tess and Frankie

'Difficulty is normal' - *Nietzsche*

With no epiphanic endings, these are unsensational lives that struggle unheroically towards normalcy; their normalcy... NS

WOBBLY TRUTHS

& Other Stories

by Natalie Scott

Contents

Safe Haven was a winner of the Hal Porter short story competition. *Dr Malady* was first published in *Meanjin, Vol. 61, No. 4.*

WOBBLY TRUTHS

& Other Stories

Foreword by Mick Le Moignan

Natalie Scott's dazzling new collection of short stories opens a window on another world – the landscape of some of our fellow-human beings that most of us prefer not to think about too deeply or too often. The heroes and heroines of these tales are simply different in a variety of ways.

The stories are not only about what happens to these characters and what they say. Conventional fiction is incidental to a piercingly perceptive insight into their innermost thoughts, the interior monologue that all of us conduct and listen to as we go about our daily business. Natalie's approach is unsentimental in the extreme – never mawkish, just the plain, cold truth, which can be as moving for the reader as it is for the characters, with its joys and moments of hilarity.

These stories are highly accomplished, mature, among the very best of their kind, perfectly formed nuggets of acutely observed mental processes, exquisite little jewels. They demand careful reading, because the tiniest well-chosen word or phrase is liable to send them rocketing off in a new direction, and you don't want to miss the ride, wherever it may take you.

The range of characters in the eleven short stories and a single novella is diverse.

The people are presented clearly, succinctly, almost objectively. The reader is allowed to make his or her own judgement: compassion is not compulsory, but the effect is to enlarge our humanity and our understanding of what it is like to be someone living on the fringes of what we consider normal life.

A final word of advice to the reader is to resist the temptation to devour several stories at a sitting. Like a fine chocolate, the maximum flavour and enjoyment is extracted when you taste them slowly. Their depth, originality and complexity make a second reading even more rewarding.

I am delighted that Natalie has agreed to *Wobbly Truths & other stories* being one of the first two titles published by Bouley Bay Books.

Safe Haven

I look at her sunny emptiness and I believe I love her.

This has been my belief for five years. Though during three of the five - against my will - sometimes I could be drawn into Sarah's fantasies.

Sunlight streams down in shafts and through the open windows the sea sucks back, then shuffles in again to our little beach rumpled with rocks which the house overlooks. The house has seen better days but, changeless... the sea sucks back, shuffles in eternally. Enclosed in the sounds and smell of it I can waste hours watching the slowness of it; it's repetition, but a varied repetition, riffled by a breeze or flattened by an offshore wind, whipped to a lace of foam, deepened by currents, slewed by countering cross currents. Yet protected by the encircling spine of the bay it seldom swells in rage. A safe haven, I was convinced when, after rattling over a huge world I met Sarah, then we bought and settled here. Beyond petrol stations and high-rise resorts and fast food, where we wanted to believe in simpler more honest things.

Colour-filled, I came to think of our lives in the colours of this place. Ever-changing blue skies, blue water, daubs of greens, yellows, reds. Until the colour went out of everything. Alice wasn't planned and Sarah was a reluctant mother whom I refused to take seriously when she proposed termination. What played in her head? Striped with shadows, perhaps I didn't know her as I thought I did. Perhaps she'd never wanted to know me.

'Why?' I implored.

Her reply: 'I'm not ready for it.'

No forewarning… neither of us was ready for our daughter's unworkable little brain encased in a seemingly normal girl child. Who could be?

~ ~ ~

Endless months with so many specialists were spent determining whether…? Over another year we consulted every known authority, registered professional or otherwise, in child development. If somewhere - deep in a cave - we'd been able to locate a hag of a witch with dark skills, we would have sought her out. Then… enmeshed in an obsession for a normal child, Sarah, who I came to see had never lifted her feet very high from the ground, was no longer one for abstractions.

'You must…' She said these two words which might have been no more than peeling skin from an orange, leaves from a bough. No pained, defenceless look, no sense of shame.

Confounded, seeping down into myself, I just leaned back in my chair and watched her. Had she sobbed I would have added sobs of my own. 'We can't change this,' I said.

'No?' If Alice's small, cone-shaped head was full of emptiness, her mother's became clogged with her brand of fantasies; nightmares in waiting for me. For both of us. Alice's baby body continued to lengthen and form in all the right places, but things became less right between her parents. It could have been as if we never looked at each other, really looked I mean, though I began to watch

Sarah. Every day. Graphic designers, we worked from home and, if not on easy street, money was not a pressing problem.

One morning Sarah made the statement I dreaded above all. Outwardly composed I took a nosedive to hell. Tanned by the sun there was a clammy pallor to her skin, her hair a tangle of kelp. She'd been walking on the beach, Alice safe with me.

She pursed her lips. To let them fall apart with: 'I wanted to abort her. You didn't.'

I surfaced. 'What!'

'So, you must…'

'NO!'

'I'm afraid…'

'We have no right to be afraid. She's ours.'

~ ~ ~

Days, weeks, slipped by as they do. Something woke me early. Between dawn and sunrise when the light is the colour of skin, Sarah was not beside me in our bed but that in itself was unalarming. Though she'd refused to breastfeed her, neither sullen nor resentful she displayed little reluctance to attend to Alice. But perfunctorily… as if her needs didn't interest her. No special smiles, none of a mother's prattling affection… her touch swift yet adequate could have been dissociated. Her work absorbed her real energies. It was my job to try and understand. And there was something more. No careless nudity now, no careless lovemaking, my wife's message was clear: I must come to terms with a single, simple child. So it was I who cradled Alice, cuddled her, felt the tiny chest tap against mine like the chest of a bird; simultaneously serene and scared by the love I experienced towards this little creature, my daughter. Serene for the rightness of some things, scared for her place in the world.

'Sarah,' I called before I moved to where Alice would be in her cot. In Sarah's day any 'bad' time came early, while for me, if I experienced depression, it tended to drop down after dark. But positive, I retained the conviction that soon Sarah's heart would mend or be devoured by an urgency to protect her child. Leave a flank unguarded, overcome the disappointment. Accept her. Time they spent together must provide a solution. Yet I was fearful of this most natural of all associations. A suspicion difficult to expel. Bleary, I knuckled my eyes, yawned. Then fully awake I saw the cot was empty. They'd be in the kitchen warming a bottle. Or... And like a man with a squint I was looking all ways at once, every image threatening, the sibilance of the sea a hiss.

When the morning cracked open with a blistering sun, I saw them from the veranda ruffled overhead by leaves. Alice laid on an outdoor table, Sarah stock-still, close, one cheek pressed against the cold metal of an axe.

Slowly, slowly with infinite care I approached, one bare foot after the other on the gravel of the path with infinite care, hands outstretched, imploring. Her name tangled, caught in my throat, refused to be released. The salt air, the sun, leached the sense out of this world of ours. Instinct told me I must not startle Sarah, precipitate action.

'Oh, there you are,' she said, then: 'Lovely morning'... and I was terrorised. She sounded normal.

I reached for the axe handle. 'Give it me.'

Sarah's laugh was raw. 'You want to do it, do you?' and with her free hand she pointed to Alice bound in a bunny rug... pink bunnies sniffing stylised daisies. Except for the bared reed of her neck, her jelly-soft little shoulders! Did she emit a bird-like cheep? What to grab? My breath pulsed into the air. The axe or the baby?

Either might trigger the worst, but with Alice in my arms she stood a better chance than the little sausage she presented on the butcher-block of the table.

Shreds of smoke flew over us as at a distance someone burned off garden rubbish; sea sounds composed, languorous... lap, lap, lap... in contrast to the battering of my heart.

'Well?'

The casual selfishness of Sarah's composure kicked off a fury towards her I didn't know I harboured.

'Get into the house,' I glowered, 'heat her bottle then put coffee on for us.'

'Okay. If that's what you want,' and looking into her eyes I had an insubstantial feeling I was seeing through her head.

~ ~ ~

We let the next day pass, then the next. I should have sought help but Sarah seemed to pass through some sort of barrier. As if she'd thrown a switch or sliced through her pillar of stone with a needle, and reason – I dare not say sanity – had returned. Sarah's teeth were very white and pearly. A month later when she smiled at me it seemed they'd grown in her mouth; painted lips drawn back from them like curtains before the performance. How could it have been possible to prepare for what she next proposed?

'You could drive her up to Wirra Wirra Lookout. On a day when the wind will lift her off the cliff and...'

A howl rose in my throat but still she smiled

'Failing that there's the exhaust pipe of the car. Or a pillow if you prefer...'

Dear God! It - the smile - must have formed in some black and awful place cramped with misery, despair. The morning should have been grey and flat and heavy but was the reverse. Brilliant with sun. Between us in her highchair, Alice fixed moist eyes on me with a kind of impersonal intensity as my fingers tightened round the coffee mug. Did her senses rocket? Mine did. Sarah's? There is scant perception - if any - in Alice, of course, only an organisation of non-functioning cells. Unimbued with curiosity... yet I would try to make up a life for her; chattering nonsense where she should have been chattering to me.

But: 'Your Mummsy-wummsy doesn't mean a word she says,' I said, a silly grin spread on my face, and as she leaned her little head sideways maybe she caught the drift. Maybe not.

Sarah's smile had scraped away. Hair thrown back and on her feet, as she flung out of the room she hurled my way: 'If you haven't the guts for what needs to be done you'd better nail your feet to the floor.'

'Nail my...?'

'So you won't have to rescue her.'

~ ~ ~

Ted, my friend since primary school and best man at our wedding, came for a short stay, his wife and twins visiting their grandmother interstate. Ted... whose age I should have been.

'Problems? Finances? Let me help out?' Ted was a generous man.

No answer from me and with Sarah off on one of her increasingly moody meanders along the beach, Ted's grip on my shoulder firmed.

'It's a shame,' he said looking at Alice, who had begun to babble.

Mashing both hands together: 'Ted,' I almost begged, 'who's she babbling to?' His shrug was slow. 'How can I help her batter her wings against her cage?' I tongued sweat off my lip. 'Get her out?'

'Sarah?' Muted questions from Ted. Had he guessed? Then on his last night when, glasses in hand, the two of us dragged chairs to the deck and watched the sun swing downwards: 'I don't like to say stupid things...' Ted crossed then uncrossed long legs, 'but I want a guarantee you'll call on me when the going gets too tough.'

~ ~ ~

Tough times, easing to calmer times, then again beach-girl Sarah's tan seemed to blanch. Suffering too much pain?

Some mornings I would wheel Alice to our local store for milk, the paper, whatever. Bowling along, old songs would trot into my head, canter out through my lips and I'd sing. Old favourites: *Me and My Gal, Summertime*, even *My Canary Has Circles Under Its Eyes*, a real old-timer my father warbled to me as a child. The sun was warm on my back. Tranquillising.

'*Oh me darling, oh me darling, oh me darling Clementine,*' I struck up - she as always curled into herself - and I skirted the pavement where hopscotch was chalked out and three small girls squealed from foot to foot. '*Not lost, but gone forever, oh me darling...*' And suddenly, blindingly, I saw a way out. Invaded by the rightness of it, my head hummed. Sarah would be released from her purgatory, freed. By me - who else?

Home again I settled Alice among her playthings, brushed lips across her cheek, her lemon-coloured hair. Her head cocked side-ways like a little hawk and for a moment she might have been regarding me with Sarah's eyes.

'Alice...?' If only something would lap between us like the waves, a breath of understanding seep through, a fleeting communication we could preserve. Perhaps there was... and I let the rest of the day pass. What did it matter what day it was? But when a sudden storm blew up followed by a stretched rainbow painting the horizon in bands of light, resilient, I recognised my wretchedness was self-indulgence, a skin to be sloughed off.

Later that week, with a determination I could not let ebb away, measuring words, I put the proposal to Sarah that she take up the lucrative offer she'd had to join a city studio.

'You mean…?'

I stared at the row of tomatoes ripening on the kitchen windowsill. 'Yes.'

After the initial disbelief - and scepticism - she seemed to spring alive. The Sarah of old, when it dawned on her she wasn't stuck fast - or forever - in the middle of her life. I was her knight-errant, I'd rescued her; the skin on my jaw tight.

The night before she was gone, we made love… and yes, I said to her repeated question, yes, I did understand. Afterwards… she was enthusiastic, proposing that maybe we could start again.

'Maybe,' my reply.

Curious, and unusual, the following morning Alice was flailing about in her cot, her hair sticky, strewn like pale seaweed on the sheet.

'Mummy had to leave early,' murmuring, I lifted her. And above her head, in the nursery mirror I saw an ashen and narrow-faced man reflected, who then carried his child to the windows which overlooked the sea. Seagulls wheeled, screeched like discordant notes, waves thwacked to the sand, the light held in rock pools like mercury. The measure of one life made scant difference to the cosmos, the inevitability of things.

'Goodbye, Mummy,' I said and was gentle, prising open her sticks of fingers to move her hand in a wave. Then no warning, rocking, she was swooping her arms.

~ ~ ~

Alice is five years old now.

I keep the enlarged photograph of Sarah - with full smile - in her room. Does Alice know this is a mother? Her mother? Know her in fuddled dreams? Wonder where's she's gone?

My head ever full of sharp pictures, I remember how I wanted to plumb this small girl's feelings later that awful day when a wind blew up, keened a lament. I hovered over her. That night, with dropping stars loose in the sky, when I tucked her tight her eyes were open... but she wasn't there within them. As usual. And as I sat beside her, I longed to gather the walls in around us, leave no room for pain. Who can tell if she carries the baggage of her mother's withheld love? Two years later and we manage. I get lots of help from our small community and Ted with his family are regular visitors.

Today, when I dress her in clean yellow socks, shirt and denim shorts, her face cocked into a smile... her smile of sunny emptiness. And smiling in turn, I love her with a bitterness that a father like me can come to know.

While the world goes about its busy way.

VISITING DOC

With his child's instinct for social dangers, Owen Perry sits silent in Doc's waiting room; Doc Harrison's.

Chin grazing his tie, he made no objection to wearing it when Nellie, who accompanies him today, suggested it. Owen thinks Nellie is old. They are actually almost the same age – but this is a thought he's unable to process. He did heave a peeved sigh when Nellie suggested he fasten his top collar button. Not that she wanted him to choke.

Doc Harrison is his GP. It's a suburban practice where neat houses are enfolded in neat gardens, few with weeds let alone ankle-length grass. Most boast annual marigolds, pansies or petunias, a clump of blue agapanthus, occasionally white. Cheerful if confined.

Owen is sort of confined... but only in his halfway house. These days he's a client of the government with a client's rights. No longer institutionalised for his own protection. Just supervised... and his ever-changing supervisors are his family. Still it has occurred to him that none of them resemble each other the way family can look on television: all with red hair or all short or fat or skinny and a mother who's always there. Every now and then at night when the light is out, he can ask himself what a mother would do, would say?

What he'd say to her? Might be like having a little dog of his own, and if he did have a dog, he'd call it Spot.

He slides a glance to Nellie. Nellie is one of an extending line of Nellies. There's also Stuart; Stuart who is happy enough to be addressed as Stuie; which is as well. His current Stuie is from somewhere in the world called Korea; the last from somewhere called Peru. He's no dummy; can tell the difference... one gives him packets of peppermints, the other takes his dinner plate away too quickly when he's not finished. He always leaves potato till last or the jam from his pudding. Apricot is his favourite, blackberry second best. Another Stuie was a hairy man, tufts of hair in his ears like ginger bird nests; 'Stirabout' his name for Owen.

'Wanna look at a maggie? The piccies?' Nellie asks, her nose down to glossy print, her hair like the hair of an old stray cat.

'Nope,' though he wonders if, in Doc's magazines on the table in his waiting room, there are some the same as Stuie's that are stacked alongside Stuie's bed. Big girls with long yellow hair, blood-red fingernails and no clothes. Not like Nellie.

'Want one?' No, he doesn't want to look at pictures; of girls or anything. Why would he when there's the fish tank against the wall with the light set behind? He turns to face it. Languid, loose... with all the time in the world two goldfish, a striped fish, a fish with a rainbow tail and a few midget fish he'd like to count, but they won't stay still to let him... slip and slop through the water. He squints. The weeds and pebbles could be shiny sweets. The sand coating the bottom of the tank looks to him like brown sugar. Gee, one day he just might be allowed to roll his sleeve up over his elbow, reach in and find out if it has the same gritty feel. Maybe... he shivers with eagerness. But for sure Owen knows that after he's seen Doc and it's time to leave, he will be able to feed the fish. Pinch his thumb and a finger into the lidded tin with the fish food, dribble it in from the top. Idly he licks his lips, wonders how it tastes; little sprinkles of roast beef or caramel chocolate? And his hand goes to his pocket. Yep, the money is safe for the *Caramello* bar when they finish here. He sucks his mouth, almost begins to taste it; syrupy sweet and the chocolate lovely glue.

A small boy trundling a wooden train from Doc's toy box, picks it up, drops it with a thud, heaves up, waddles towards the fish tank. Owen is displeased. With a sudden mood lurch, he glowers. Doc's tank and the fish should be his for the time he waits. He doesn't want to own them, but the intruder should go back to the toy box. Better if he altogether disappeared... but diversion is at hand.

'Listen to this one,' an old fellow, who has one leg instead of two, bellows at his companion, chortles. 'Haitch for 'Arrison,' Little response. 'Listen. Haitch an' a hay, two hars, a hi, a hess, a ho an' a hen. Get it?' he trumpets. 'Arrison.'

Owen stares at the idiot. 'Idjit,' he reports to Nellie, Nellie to nod, yawn. 'Idjit' is a familiar word, one which seems to echo to him from long ago. 'Idjit,' he repeats to Nellie with satisfaction and again she nods. Nodding Nellie, he thinks, sniggers a bit. He frowns, tugs his head sideways. Did she tell him he was to open his mouth wide as a shark today? Say: aaah! Can't remember, can't remember... and his tongue goes big in his mouth.

Then Doc appears, signals in the woman and the child, gives a wave to Owen who presses his knees together over his hands. Again he is absorbed with the fish, wonders how it would be swimming with them in their green world. The bubbles from the pipe might bubble him to the surface, bubble him right out of the tank. Through the air, through the ceiling, through the roof. Where then? Through the sky, over mountains. Then? Owen wriggles in delight. To a big lagoon where birds skim over the water. Where frogs croak and...

'Mr Owen Perry...' and startled, he hears his name. Any threat recedes. Gee, it's only Doc with his great joke. Mr Owen Perry! Doesn't he always give him the full name... 'the full moniker,' one Nellie mystifyingly kept explaining, but she made no sense to him at all.

'Mr Owen Perry,' is repeated and Mr Owen Perry tingles with delight. No 'you' or 'kid' or 'fella' here.

Both he and Nellie stand, she joggles his arm and he gives his reply... his regular reply. 'Righty-oh, Doc HARRISON.' He never forgets the other half of the joke. But once through the door he wants everything to go back to how it was in the waiting room. Here the light is too bright, and there are funny things beside the high bed with its sheet so white it makes him think of... of something he can't remember.

'How are you, Owen, how have you been?' he, Owen, is asked, but when Nellie does the answering, he groans. This is the way to make Doc turn directly to him and he wants to smile but somehow can't... the smile driven away off into a corner. His hands fist, his lower lip tremors. Deep down in him there's a sort of tearing and he doesn't want to blub like a kid. But he does... a bit. Tight-throated, tight-chested, he gets a picture in his head of that little kid who was outside but came inside here. First. Before his turn. Dressed in green and red like a bird. A green-red parrot with a sparrow face. That kid... who had a mother with him who led him by the hand.

~ ~ ~

Unbeknown to Owen, Dr Harrison thinks of that child, the patient he ushered in previous to Owen's appointment. Shy as he clung to his mother, it was necessary to win his trust. Naturally he's well practised. When the squeezed yellow duck failed, he'd reached into a drawer for the new distracting toy. A wind-up kangaroo, the jointed plastic legs ready to hoppity-hop over his desk between this week's pharmaceutical samples and the prescription pad. It did the trick, the child's eyes luminous, the soft mouth agape.

Stuck for moments in his line of thought: I'll suggest a second opinion, he's reminding himself, if the tests aren't what I expect. Then he shrugs alert to Owen Perry, thumbs through his notes, inclines his head down and reveals to Owen a bald patch the colour of sand, which he'd like to stroke.

'Had any dizziness since your last visit, Owen?' he asks. Owen has just left forty behind and has a history of erratic blood pressure. No reply. 'Owen?'

'He...' Today's carer, Nellie, begins, but Doc raises his right palm to her.

'Owen, you tell me...' But it's clear that Owen, if mildly, is distressed. On occasions on previous visits he's displayed agitation; not unlike his last patient, the child.

'Owen?'

But Owen barely hears his name over the whump which sounds like a muffled truck in his chest, while Nellie bristles a bit and creases her face up more.

'Not to worry, Owen. You're fit as a flea.'

'Yep?'

'Yep,' and before he reaches for the kangaroo, Dr Harrison gives him one of his warm smiles. Where's the damn key. Aah... and he turns it. Clickety-click.

Next… hoppity-hop… and the kangaroo leaps in circles.

Dr Harrison repeats the exercise. Again. Owen narrows his eyes, leans forward, leans back, pulls his fingers one by one. He doesn't want things spoiled between himself and Doc. But… Unwilling, he turns to Nellie, just does, and swallows hard.

'Want to see it hop again?' Nellie, all patience - or pretending - isn't keen to waste time. Doesn't she have to note any ailment, let alone new medication or change of pills in the daybook before the end of her shift?

Re-facing Doc, something now sort of rattling in his throat, Owen's expression might be disgust. Up go his hands in the air; one to either side of his ears. He circles both index fingers before jabbingly he points to Doc… a grown man playing with that silly thing.

'Idjit.'

'What's that, you say, Owen?'

Relaxed now, Owen is happy to repeat, emits a croak of a laugh. 'Idjit.'

'Idjit?' And Doc pushes aside the kangaroo to poke at his own chest, presses his lips together, hiding his teeth.

'Yep.'

Brow crinkling up, appearing and feeling foolish, Dr Harrison is forced to agree. 'Okay if this idjit takes your blood pressure, Owen?' he laughs.

'Yep, Doc…'

'Good.'

And Owen begins to hum with a sense of whatever it is that he can hum with here; layered between what seem to be giant cushions of cotton wool which smell as if they've been powdered with baby talc. Nice.

'Righty-oh, Doc,' he thrusts forth his arm from his high-rolled sleeve. And attentive, he watches Doc's hands, as in established routine the black bandage is taken out of the same long box as always... Then next the strings are uncoiled. They always make Owen think of licorice. He can almost taste it.

BALANCING THE BOOKS

For seven years I thought I'd divorce my husband. Now there's not the need. We had our season. Which has come to an end. I've indulged in daydreams where I tolerated his abject boredom, so all-suffocating it could have induced some women to hurl themselves over a cliff. No excuses; he'd not even had the blessing of an unhappy childhood.

Joel-James Percival was all the children his doting parents wanted. Was that why his mind was so circumscribed, cramped? Their loopy arms circled about him like a moat keeping the rest of the world at bay. Not that they were disagreeable let alone biased against me; who came to see myself as the drawbridge lowered for his escape. You see, his mother may have been twisted, insane, but I'm not about to spit on her memory.

'Joel-James is suggestible,' she confided in the coppery afternoon light on our first meeting. Which was to prove the last. Fingers like bony twigs, she handed me the Royal Doulton cup, saucer and plate aligned with cake fork, then a slice of the festive gateau. Her rouged cheeks were beacon-like with what she must have considered bold – but essential – information to disclose to a future daughter-in-law. 'Suggestible,' she repeated, eyes a-glitter to lean back into the support of her chair while Joel-James sat forward, smiled his sunny smile as if something had been confirmed. 'He enjoys being told what to do.' Emphasis was laid on 'enjoys'.

Perfect, I thought, after bruisingly having loved Philip, young as I was then and star-struck; Philip a theatre man. Who in theatre parlance: 'did me wrong'. Verbally violent, bullying with his insistence that he think for us both AND I was to jump to it, quick smart. Which I did because backstage ran the rumour that a former lover had quit Philip with the legacy of a splayed nose.

'Dawn,' was whispered to me, 'be warned.'

Still there was a real gain. Unaware of it, Philip taught me to become the consummate actor I am; good at public faces, concealing what I feel. What I came to feel with Philip was a wanting to be somewhere else.

The same followed with Joel-James, history repeating itself as many a know-all pontificates. Yet Joel-James was capable of leading me by the hand through a certain topic. Figures, yes, strange, but given to soft laughter he thrived on adding, multiplying, subtracting... balancing imagined books... while, at forty – my junior by five years – he had a lifetime of growing up to do. For starters: setting his own agenda. Let alone choosing his clothes. His mother's choice was neat and neutral for her boy, but there was the addition of his father's regimental stripes for Joel-James' ties where strident blues and purples and gold warred with the browns, the greys. Joel-James did, said, wore, ate, etc, whatever one or other – quiet but batty – stated should be his mode of life. Dear God, cracked into my head more than once, was I destined to take over their role? Why? Because after meeting and approving me they up and died. Took wings, escaped... what you will. Joined the crowd in the sky, passing their guardianship on to me. Who immediately lopped Joel-James to Joel.

~ ~ ~

Me: I'm strong and strong-willed. With the blessing of an unhappy childhood you either sink or swim. Sink or swim... rise or fall... weak as water... strong as an ox. Don't the clichés say it all?

When I met Joel, I felt: take it or leave it... but further acquaintance revealed that his smothering parents were rich. Very rich. Cushioned by money since birth, despite an interest in figures, Joel set little store on this, which does seem incredible, doesn't it? Odd, but when you're penniless you scheme for money. Owning little you yearn to be cluttered with stuff: real estate, shares, high credit ratings... But when – via Joel – I acquired heaps, my schemes changed; I spent with relish on whatever I fancied.

The hardship of my childhood began to recede. Too little money, too little love, too many siblings. A harridan of a mother who took to drink with a feckless father. A poor diet and not enough of it; sometimes I've thought they could have cooked the cockroaches, made up a big pot of stew. Such a childhood is best left behind. We kids all went our separate ways, but one memory I retained was the memory of sound. The banging of feet and everything else that clattered on our bare floorboards. Scarred and unswept. Maybe this explains why, on introduction to Joel's parents, I almost felt the cost of the carpets burning through my shoes. Plus a thrill to think of money in the bank, if not mine. In high and airy rooms where extravagant lights replaced the naked bulbs of my early life which hung on fly-blown cords. You don't disremember details like that. Also blessed – or cursed – by an intense sense of smell, which in my newly perfumed adult life I prefer not to awaken.

'Joel, dear, do this, or that...' and unerringly Joel complied. Face folding into a smile, no flared nostrils, no grimaces, grunts or shrugged shoulders, his was a sunny disposition. Yet no fool, Joel was alert enough with his glossy brown eyes, even though less endearing were his flattened features, horse-like laugh, his hairy hands.

After Philip I suppose I wanted a life without complications. Minus the manic rages, let alone the daily tantrumettes; public exuberance, private hell. But… promises, promises, silly me, at last I dropped to the fact that Philip did not intend me for stardom, presenting his Trilby to a world waiting to applaud my talent. *Par excellence*. As I say, I learned to act. Which continues to hold me in good stead.

When we married, what a chance Joel had to make something new of himself! Money plentiful, he had no need to work. With his parent's recommendation to follow his bent – which came down to a sort of hobby accountancy – of course he agreed. But… I put to him that there were more exciting ways to spend a life. Unselfish, I tried to re-invent him, and, as a further *cliché* goes, to expand his horizons. Shit… apart from stamp collecting all I managed to snare his interest in was swimming. He never swam as a boy.

Medium tall but thick-waisted, it was child's play to persuade him to take it up for reasons of health. More important was to get him out of the house. Waking hours and he liked nothing but to respond to suggestions; cloaked orders from me. I admit I didn't have to suggest he clean his teeth but should I have done so… Sex? Yes, as ever he was obliging, but, nose jutting to the ceiling, he preferred to settle for the abandonment of sleep. Needless to say, he snored.

Entrusted as he was to me, I refused to make his parents' mansion our home. Arches, ironwork, rooms dim with umber depths, topped by a witches' hat of a turret, filled with their rich things. I'd not be comfortable there.

'Well?' slack-jawed, never reproachful, Joel allotted me near-divinatory powers.

So we live on the spread of a deep lagoon with sweeping views. The lagoon empties into the sea. Spending up I avoided the vulgarity and showiness of those who employ a decorator where the results are shop displays. Peopled by Dawn and Joel... Joel outfitted in the clothes I select for him. Boredom, *ennui*; sometimes, with justification this can be laid at one's own doorstep, but I don't lack resources, never have. Dullness isn't only defined as no-colour, off-colour, pasty-pale. Can be fire-engine red. Maddening. Wearied to the point of extinction by the tedium of this man, there've been occasions I've come close to decamping. Cashing in my chips.

But to return to the swimming.

'Joel,' I smiled like a hovering parent after he learned to tread water, dog paddle, breaststroke, the dome of his belly less convex when he floated on his back. Graduating to over-arm: 'Test yourself' I slid into his mind.

Did he throw me a sharp look? No... just his slicked tongue over his teeth. 'Got any suggestion?'

Well, yes, I had. 'Why not venture out further into the lagoon each day? Towards the first marker buoy of the channel...'

'You mean...?' he looked askance and I felt a little out of breath. Did I sense mutiny when – for moments – I fancied he'd not agree? Man the barricades?

Joel didn't rebel. Proficient now with the Aussie crawl, it was a pleasure to reward him. The wrist-o-meter measured his distance, while the measure of his pleasure was my reward. Delighted too by my proposal to keep a daily record of his progress in a leather-bound notebook. Eager to please, each day he'd swim a little farther, while each day I checked the coastal weather conditions. Secretly. Fed by experience, I suppose this started with speculation as to how far he'd go on my suggestion or authorisation. And if I faltered it wasn't for long. Towel to hand, notebook to pocket, I'd wait on the sandy patch at the bottom of our lawn which tilted to the lagoon. Until the increasingly distant speck, which was Joel, returned.

'My plucky hero,' I'd call as breathing hard he'd flop to land, his goggled eyes like fish, the mix of his body odour – strong and highly individual – combined with the tang of salt. I've often regretted the acuteness of my sense of smell – but I've learned to put it out of my mind. My plucky hero! Yes, my voice – but it began to sound a manufactured voice. I guess this was a curious, if unorthodox, strategy to plan to be alone which few would understand. Except someone going batty in the presence of the boringly dead... undead.

So the year went on. Joel less blubbery, less winded, the level of his fitness on the increase. Also on the increase was local interest. At the pub there was talk of cutting down on beer, giving up ciggies and competing with Joel, or just swimming along. This did not please me. His regime must be accelerated. Atmospheric conditions and weather changes became an obsession. Stratosphere, tropopause. Warm fronts, cold. Occlusions, air movements, areas of frontal cloud sheets, isobars. Forecasts... Balancing cirrostratus with cumulonimbus then gradient wind, I prepared.

The morning was dazzling, perfect. Shading my eyes against the sun, I cooed 'Joel, I've a wonderful idea.' Did my voice sound an imitation of a voice? But no need to stall.

'Yes?' a half grin twitched.

Flattery another weapon, I weighted it with emphasis. 'You ARE an amazing swimmer. Tremendous. You've taken to it like…'

'A duck to water?'

'A duck? Yes, that, but I'd say a champion.'

'You mean it?' His voice had a catarrhal rasp. I nodded hard, smiled and the smile seemed fixed. 'Make it to the far marker,' and patted his chest with my free hand. We'd celebrate with a bottle of *Veuve Cliquot*. No cheap bubbly *Great Western* or *Carrington's* for this occasion.

As usual, like the encouraging parent I'd become, I accompanied him to the water's edge. Warm salt breeze, the sky throbbed blue, the air crystalline. A more perfect morning may never have dawned. A trickle of waves lapped to shore and lumpy sand under my feet I smoothed back his hair, checked his wrist-o-meter. Then as usual, he was awaiting starting orders. As if I held a gun in my hand. 'Off with you!' I said.

A whinny of a laugh, a splash and in he went, ruffling the platter of the lagoon. A solitary seagull swooped, cried overhead, wheeled away. I felt my sneakers wet, then my knees, my thighs, cold layering my skin.

'Joel…' I called before I barked the order: 'Come back!' My fist pushed against my ribs. 'Come back, do you hear?'… but his furrowing body was parting the water which closed after him. Seamlessly. Changed from green to dark blue. What have I done?

~ ~ ~

Drawing back the folds of the curtains with a diagonal sweep there was our familiar, yet unaccountably unfamiliar view. In mingled wonder I watched as Joel telescoped to a speck. Dull, tedious Joel… a speck fated to disappear.

An hour later I was sure none of this was happening. A fevered stillness in a sudden brooding light, then the atmospheric racket kicked in. Emptied of everything but a pewter glow soon to be split by lightning, before the thunder broke through, crashed, rumbled to a roar. Then somewhere something rattled, and everything was interwoven in sheets of rain.

~ ~ ~

No figure in the landscape. The seascape.

'Are you living your own real life?' burbled to me from the radio. Above this elemental fury I had to connect to a human voice.

Living my own real life? Tomorrow when the storm leaves the lagoon washed flat and blue with another day, how shall I be left? But today's not yet over… and I've come through so far. No one can pin it on me. Suggesting is no crime. If it were, what or who can offer proof? My hand trembles when I reach for the binoculars but don't lift them. Instead I lift the *Veuve Cliquot*. Still chill on the tray I set out earlier: the champagne, Joel's favourite cheese, crackers, one glass. A massive sigh and pulling away the foil and wire cap I twist the cork. Pop! Tilt the bottle, pour.

Radio pips synchronise with the chimes from the grandfather clock I believed it right that Joel bring with us here from his old home. Hadn't he heard this same clock striking off the hours during his many formative years?

So… aghast yet excited… 'Dawn,' I instruct myself, 'time to call the police.' Then, poised if tense, I must manage their impassive expressions which – all in a day's work – are prone to follow the standard statement of sympathy. My role of widow is well rehearsed.

Should his drowned body be recovered or drift back or be washed up by a receding tide, how appropriate if it's draped with seaweed. Dark seaweed, preferably black. A pity the wet suit I ordered hadn't been delivered... and for moments I see Joel sleek as a porpoise. The store will take it back, refund my account... but I must refuse the picture of a bruised or bloated face, sunken eyes.

What might be a final crack of thunder bursts. The house goes black. With power gone, when will it be restored? The front door flies open. And my flesh creeps. Dear God... you're someone I seldom entreat... but what IS that smell? Imagination? My nose twitches: no. Stronger and stronger... awful... an enveloping enemy. Ever sensitive to smell, I could be drowning in it, gulping, labouring to breathe.

His – Joel's body odour strong, individual – combined with a salt tang of the sea! A rush of saliva fills my mouth.

WHO – AND FROM WHERE – IS SUGGESTING THIS TO ME?

MOTHER'S DAY

He clenches his hands, clenches them tighter.

'Shaun,' Marika is saying, then again saying something that doesn't appear to mean anything to him. But... does. His breath becomes raggedy. In the way it can for him with pets – a guinea pig, a rabbit – except with pets he can be shot through with fuzziness, a warmth.

'Her day's come round again. HER day,' she emphasises, 'Mother's Day.' Now she sniffs the stale air in Shaun's room, where the furniture looks planted in the brown carpet: bed, upright chair, wardrobe, table. Functional, with the sturdy pine table where one by one with meticulous concentration he paints battalions of toy soldiers. These he stores militarily in a box under his bed. Shaun who is sixteen has been domiciled here at Waratah House for four years and in institutions elsewhere since his second birthday.

Moving to the window, Marika heaves up the pane of glass and throws her arms out from her shoulders like an impresario. From the low hill on which the building stands the view is pleasing. Edging suburbia, there are still puffs of green that are trees, birds, open spaces, though more and more blocks and spec-built houses are being offered for sale where the billboards shout:

Desirable Family Residences close to Schools.

New Shopping Mall, Amenities and Sporting Facilities.

Like strips of tinsel the morning sun catches on a metal roof, tops a wire fence.

'Mothering Sunday.' Marika sort of sings. 'That's what it's called where I come from.' She turns to the gawky boy. 'England, you know.'

Shaun nods. Not forceful but with little jerks and Marika thinks what she's unerringly thought since she first came to help out as a volunteer in this house run by the Department. No dummy, far from it, this boy is diagnosed: MUTE. Shaun Caulfield, whose files record: *'Non-verbal. Does not emit articulate sounds. Hearing normal so restrictedly educable'*. Pages of medical data follow. Diagnoses. *'Prognosis: not good'*. Marika folds his pyjamas, slips them under his pillow.

'Shaun?' Marika thinks he's trying to smile. And she in turn smiles into his lovely eyes: big, round, a melting brown. 'Shaun,' she repeats, 'SHE will be here to see you today.' But he drifts away from her voice. Is he inching back in time? To a mother he knew briefly? Very briefly. Though who can tell what – if any – threads cling. Marika furrows her brow. Can it be that his dislocation, his baby pain, was so encompassing that he continues to hide from language? A silence he can't – or won't – crack?

'I expect she has plans to take you out,' she says. And if his eyes seem to acquire a haunted look, Marika's voice gathers speed. 'Just for a while. Somewhere nice; somewhere you'll enjoy.' Though she can't imagine where he'd want to go with his mother, a stranger on an annual visit to a son, it has been noted, which on no occasion has extended beyond two hours. Marika has never seen Mrs. Caulfield… or whatever name she goes by… but it's said that it's obvious the woman has money. Well-dressed and bejewelled, she comes bearing gifts. Marika pulls her mouth tight, draws her chin down; extravagant clothes so it would seem that superficial appearances matter to her, even if she's unable to gauge his size from one year to the next. Can Shaun gauge who she is? Does instinct inform him? Guide him?

'Shaun?'

The boy's response is to huddle into himself then shuffle to his table. It's what he does. No layers of words. Does he think or feel his thoughts, as now from the table's one drawer he pulls out his box of paints, inks and brushes? Next a compact, tissue-wrapped parcel, the tissue whispering as he removes it with careful hands. It's a Cromwellian Trooper in half-armour. And stretching the wings of his nose he smells its lobster-tail helmet, draws it into the orbit of his life with what must be pleasure.

'Shaun?' she begins again and there's a tangy smell when he uncorks a bottle of lacquer, maybe glue, unscrews several pots of paint, aligns them with a jar which holds fine-tipped brushes. Marika would rather leave him be, but: 'You've showered this morning? Put on clean underpants? T-shirt?' He nods, slopes a shoulder and thrusts a foot out at her. She could understand if he was angry, or at least disparaging. But he's not. 'Socks, too. Good boy.' Good boy! 'That's great,' she adds. Then somehow, she wants to add: 'Thank you'.

~ ~ ~

Marika studies the woman as she pushes through the glass doors, approaches the front desk. Disquieting, yet in an odd way alluring, it has to be her. Medium height, sleek but square-shouldered, she wears grey: pigeon grey, a lorikeet-coloured scarf knotted silkily at the throat about a gold necklace, under long gold earrings. And 'rich bitch'… Marika thinks, noting the glossed if pinched lips, the straight blonde hair. And finds that she herself feels dowdy.

One shoulder pulled a bit to one side by the capacious – and named – carrier bags she holds, the woman sighs. In self-concern? Or is it? What? Marika cannot know, but does know that right now she's as judgemental as hell. Is this unfair? She doubts it and so is not forthcoming with the normal enquiry but waits.

No confusion, no anguish: 'Would you direct me to Shaun Caulfield.'

But Marika is anguished if not confused. 'Are you a relative?'

'I am?'

'A close relative?'

The voice is unbruised. 'His mother.'

Marika wants to demand identification, but: 'Oh,' she says with a stillness she does not feel; could leap at this woman's gilded throat. Instead she straightens papers which don't need straightening, her mouth tight. 'Then you'll know where to find him.'

'No,' Shaun's mother's response is blunt, and there's nothing to do but lead her to Room 11. She won't even try to force a smile. Along the corridors the light is split between shade and striped sunshine through the barred windows. No prison, Waratah House has been constructed to protect those unable to protect themselves. Only the linoleum is drained of colour, the honey-white of the walls hung with prints. It's not an unreasonable place to live and staff are expected not to noisily lose their tempers.

The door to Shaun's room is ajar and though madam may be inclined to barge in, Marika knocks. Once again. 'Can we come in? As if caught up in some pervading unlocalised ache, for a moment he looks like a boy she doesn't know and her voice quavers in sympathy. 'Shaun, your visitor has come.'

32

'His mother has come,' says the woman with emphasis, as if it's a key which not only gives her right of entry, but rights to all she has done or not done over the past sixteen years. Exonerated!

Marika snorts: as if SHE'S entitled to some gesture of recognition. But Shaun's pallor alarms Marika. Can his mind's eye assemble a mother? Then colour spreads up from his neck to his ears as his mother steps to him. No detonation of identification, at her touch there could be knives going through his hand as he clutches it away, stands back.

'You can leave us,' Marika is told, who has no intention of doing so.

'No,' she states with a firmness that surprises her, gathers the skirt of her uniform and hefts herself up onto a space at the end of Shaun's table, leaving the chair for the visitor if she wishes to be seated. She does, and it occurs to Marika that she must sit her out till the situation improves, Shaun less stressed. Then folding her arms it occurs to her that she, who abhors violence, could wind up a fist and deliver a punch to defend this boy.

Now with a speculative glance at her son, then to the carrier bags beside her stylishly shod feet, the woman begins what may be a practised overture but probably only reflects her interest in 'things'. She smiles, her tongue showing a bit, then: 'I've brought you pressies, sweetie. Lovely pressies.' She's close to batting her lashes. 'Don't you want to see them?" His head plunges down but she's not deterred. 'I guarantee you'll just love them. Come and unwrap them,' the voice trills, 'then you can tell me what you think.'

'What?' For a moment Marika longs to slap her face.

The woman droops with laughter; sounds which lap like small waves against the walls of her son's room and her son's bony body, his helplessness.

'Shaun,' Marika murmurs, desperate for diversion and hating the deception, 'maybe your mother's brought you a *Hussar Trumpeter*, maybe a *Prince of Wales Lancer*.' For she must distil the tension, lead him back to himself. He looks to her and she tries to nod, then as if alive with opportunities of ancient military toys, she sees him relax. A little. To a troubled excitement. Surely this awful woman has at least included chocolates.

'The pressies,' the woman prompts. Then sotto voce: 'Though it IS Mother's Day.'

Shaun knuckles his eyes, then with angular gestures closes the distance between them. No, not them, but the carrier bags which have been nudged his way. No sound from the women who watch, he yanks at the parcels. Systematic, emptying the carrier bags, he searches for what is not there. No *Lancers*, no *Hussars*. There are a pair of Italian loafers which may or not fit, a blue shirt, a yellow shirt, a Hawaiian shirt with coconuts, fronds of palm trees, jeans and a linen jacket, unsuitably cream.

'Shaun?'

Shaun's eyes turn glassy, angry, while Mrs. Caulfield's eyes shade with what could be a different anger as each item hits the floor. But she will not have her gifts dismissed, and a hollowness strikes Marika as Mrs. Caulfield hits the air close to Shaun's shoulders.

'After all the goddamn time I spent shopping for you, the least you can do is try them on,' she says as she strips cellophane from one of the shirts, pushes it at his chest.

Pulled on and buttoned, it's so oversized it would have taken half another boy. He pats the pockets with his fingers. Nothing there. Then as she reaches for the jeans, Marika knows she will object if the woman as much as attempts to unzip the faded trousers Shaun wears. Outraged, is it possible that he is turning over his words; condemned to keep the sound of them strangled somewhere between brain and tongue?

Mrs. Caulfield – or whoever she is – throws up her eyes and sighs. 'Sixteen. You should have filled out by now,' she declares. Indignantly? As if some actor in her head had been playing the part of her son, cast in the role to meet her annual seat at his performance. An actor with no lines, no speaking part.

Marika makes a click with her teeth. Something snaps under Shaun's heel as he retreats; a plastic covered razor. Had she expected his downy-soft skin to bristle with a man's stubble?

'Try on the jacket.' If not a peremptory order, it is an order.

Marika picks it up, shakes it, helps him shoulder into it. Hands in the pockets, he flaps them against his hips.

With a sigh of exasperation she says: 'I suppose you can wear that as we're going out,' before she manages to infer that by some transgression he hasn't accommodated his size to her shopping. 'Anyone would have supposed you'd have filled out more.'

Anyone! Marika stifles withering accusations, angry tears. In this room, breathing the same air as this svelte creature, she feels shamed. What can she do? Jump up and down? Tell her to leave and leave Shaun alone? Leave him to those who attend to him, care for him? But they are leaving. Is his expression amazement? Or passivity in the face of defeat?

'We're off for a good time,' is thrown over a departing shoulder to Marika. 'A good time and a good chat.'

~ ~ ~

The sun is strong, laps about them as she leads him through the grounds to the gate, where beyond the high fence a taxi waits. Against the light the sun shines through her clothes and outlines the shape of her body. Woman-shaped, different. In the taxi he squirms away from her, sucks the back of his hand, looks out the window.

'There's a football field,' she declares and as they swerve alongside then pass it, he doesn't see a foot or a ball. Just grass. Green like the green he uses for some of his soldiers. And glancing at his hands he derives what could be comfort from his thumb nail smudged with paint. Khaki, army green.

She sniffs queenly, says: 'So this is YOUR new shopping mall,' and wary, he sidles between displays floating in a gauzy haze which interest him less than the things she brought him. So many, so many, and the revolving lights set him blinking.

He stumbles against a pudgy child who sets up a wail, backs away. But not before a woman yelps like a dog, and he's baffled, feels a deep dislike for everything.

'Mind where you put your big clumsy feet.' A man takes up a stance in front of him, peers at him, face nasty. 'How about an apology. Lost our tongue, have we?'

Now the woman who brought him here in the taxi wedges herself between them. She's pinkened by rosy lights and he smells the smell of her that came with her into his room earlier.

'Piss off,' issues from her mouth and the man steps aside and is soon lost in shapes which crouch everywhere. 'Come on,' she turns, but alien sensations race round him. Sounds are jumping, sights swirl and slither too near. Something fatly plops from a machine and as he watches it she's suggesting that he does not want a doughnut. 'We'll eat well. Upstairs,' she states, 'I've a reservation,' and with grudging steps he follows her.

~ ~ ~

36

As if they've passed from one world to another, he sits opposite her, a table between them wrapped in a white cloth.

'This is better,' and she settles to the wine she's ordered. There's juice for him.

He gives himself a sort of shake and his hair fans across his forehead. When she reaches over to smooth it back he jerks away, but with less vehemence than he retreated from her touch in his room. A girl appears with pad and pencil to take their order, and, head low, he begins to lick the web of skin between one index finger and thumb. She'll have an omelette with garden herbs, she tells the waitress. Fresh, she insists. To follow; the salmon.

'And for the young man?'

'What do they usually eat?' she questions the surprised girl in rounded syllables, but: 'No, no,' is her response to the gourmet hamburger, potato wedges, and she proceeds to order several dishes. Then, when the waitress suggests this is rather a lot, and maybe thinks extravagant as well as wasteful: 'Just bring it.' Then she adds the potato wedges and the hamburger.

No smoking, but she lights a cigarette. Several quick puffs at it then she grinds it out but the lingering smoke makes his eyes water. Briefly she closes her own eyes before staring at him. He doesn't like this.

Then: 'What rattles round in your head?' she questions him with a throaty noise which might be a laugh… but all he hears is a storm of sound as a leggy girl adjusts then cuts the volume on her device. Next she's showing him a photo. It is her, but she's harder, sharper somehow and the hair is longer. Unnerved, he looks to other tables where people are eating with younger and older women who could be having a good time. Happy? Well… they're smiling. Unwrapping parcels. Sniffing flowers.

Is he happening here? Wiping his eyes with the back of his hand, a dish sizzles past and his mouth floods with saliva. When his food arrives, — and there's lots of it — he must be happening here... and... maybe someone has slid in to sit with him; someone familiar.

~ ~ ~

Two women and a small girl crooning to her dolly vacate the taxi which Shaun and his mother then take. Beside her in this afternoon light he can see her skin hardening into patterns, her hair bright wire. He sucks in his teeth. If he ran off in a circle, then ran back, would he meet himself? Where he belongs? How he wants to run off, even if some itch of a thing makes him want to stay. Outside Waratah House he toes the ground, then kicks at a stone while she pays the driver. About to accompany him to the gates — as she must — she decides to have the taxi wait. She straightens the scarf, primps the wire hair. 'Ten minutes. At most,' she drawls.

Then it's her he wants to kick, not the stone. Spit at her too. Kick, spit, kick, spit... With her trill of a laugh followed by: 'Don't we always have a day of fun together?' he does spit. Gathers another gob. Again.

'Shaun!'

All he does now is stare beyond her. Next he paces away. Doesn't turn. More steps and he breaks into a clumsy run before the over-large jacket flaps like wings. He flies up the slope. Away from her. Off the path, out of her sight, things rush to fill a hollow inside him. Yelps, jagged sobs... And at the top he trips. Face in the earth, he doesn't lift it. Then bit by bit the cords of his neck loosen... and bit by bit his spread arms reach further to stake out his territory. Like a fallen soldier.

~ ~ ~

Marika asks herself if there could be a different way of talking to the world. A silent way. Shaun is asleep in his room. The questionable Mrs. Caulfield has been gone for hours. This visit – which will be entered in the daybook then in Shaun's files – was forty-five minutes longer than any previous visit. Fifteen of which were spent in the front office waiting for a taxi.

Is it possible that this woman has set up so deep a trauma in Shaun that his grief would not pass? His experiences always masked by silence? No. 'Always' is an inadmissible word for Marika, 'Never' another. She snorts as her heart thuds with vexation, grief. Where is her objectivity? Diffident, she had offered the woman tea.

Had the mouth twitched? The eyes shaded with anxiety? 'Anything stronger?'

'Afraid not. No.' Marika's lips felt bone dry.

'Then tea it must be.'

Nothing soft or yielding seemed attached to the woman. Marika experienced an obscure revulsion. Yet she was trapped into sympathy – a modicum of sympathy – with the tremor in the woman's hand when she took the cup, emptied it, then the way she began to chaff her braceleted wrists after she replaced it on the tray. Did the face contain sadness? Even when re-enamelled with make-up? A longing for what could never be? Shaun's existence her heartbreak?

Marika feels diminished; hands in pockets tightens her cardigan around her hips. No. This woman struck her as someone who could well hate what she had while she envied what she didn't have. Or maybe had lost. What mother – by an appearance once a year – could submit her child to so distorted a rebirth? This was bizarre.

Obscene. A child still at sixteen, becalmed in his speechless world; unable to give tongue to an aloneness few are forced to understand.

'Goodnight,' Marika calls at the staff room door.

'Good night, good night,' they call to her and out she goes to make her way to her car. Low clouds, the sky unjabbed by stars, it's a dark night. She heaves her shoulders, sighs. Darkness suspends everything. She sighs again. Until tomorrow...

Somewhere a dog barks. She fits her key into the lock, slides in along the seat, starts the engine. Then hands set high on the wheel takes her road home. In silence.

DR MALADY

These are his rooms. His domain. Here he sets the boundaries. Or breaks them.

Seated opposite him she's saying: "I was going into this tiny room at the end of the world.'

'Yes?'

'No windows. Tiny. Two feet by four,' she specifies.

'You knew the measurements?' And she sucks a sob down to her stomach, and of course he waits.

Weekdays – 8am to 12, 2pm to 5, with the exception of golfing Wednesday, seminars, conferences, meetings, holidays at home or abroad – his language is mostly silence.

'Yes,' she whispers.

Outside the day whispers. Whispers with rain. Pain? Earlier the sun was sheeted by cloud which by midday had taken on a metallic tinge. Loose drops kicked down then joined to a beaded curtain, which rustles now, softly audible. With a smell of sadness. Sadness! Never inconvenienced by self-distrust, he braces his shoulders, allows his lips to broaden – slightly – a creature of masks before he subsides into the leather of his chair once more. Does the air stir? Maybe he's caught this smell of sadness from…?

He adjusts his glasses, gives a jut to his nose. Deborah, yes, Deborah. He's been seeing her for years with her lip-sticky voice which can turn gratingly tiresome. Or strangled, tied up in her bundles of memories as she fights her helplessness. Her Thursday helplessness. If he wants to sigh he does not want it observed. After all, to survive requires obstinacy.

'What does this dream convey to you?'

She's terse. 'You're the expert, you tell me.'

Dearie me... misjudged the timing. 'This tiny room? Was it dark?'

'Dark?'

'Shadowed, grey, blue-black, black?'

'As black as...' but she props, hands rigid on the swell of her thighs, unwilling to appear racist, intolerant, swishing further words round in her mouth. Then swallowing them, her protuberant eyes bulged over, for moments sightless behind lids feathered by veins.

'It was a warm place.' She can't or won't say more.

So: 'A warm place where you were taken care of,' he suggests, weighing his voice as if it's a measure of sugar to sweeten milk.

'That's a lot of words from you,' she quips in a defence which she hopes sounds funny. Does not. But wary, her eyes watch him, the tension breaks and her lips could be hurting with the effort to hold in everything she has to say. It seems he's opened the floodgates. Nodding encouragement, mute, he reckons how long before her fifty minutes are up. When from a prudent mouth he'll roll: 'Till next week.' Deborah... Vicki, Marguerite, Sheena, Patsy... Some colleagues ring a little bell. Now the rain which slaps hard against the windows has nothing to do with her. Nothing.

The edges of that wet day come back to him in waves. His chest heaves, his heart thumps. It was long ago. Forty-two years. Brief by human counting.

In yellowy darkness, he could have dammed up the gutter to a deeper puddle if he'd been able to locate more bricks. There'd been a pile of them under the railway bridge but some kid - or someone - had spirited them away. He'd spit in his eye if it was Kit.

A heady day; hadn't he told Kit after he'd jumped the ditch and stumbled on them? Under a rotting sheet of canvas smelling like fish? Kit's thumbs may be double-jointed and he may be able pick up things with his toes, but he jumps higher, bends wire further ... so they'd share. Together hurl the bricks at enemies, construct a fort, block the gutter in a storm and trap what floated down? Kit - smaller but older - would spit back at him sharp as a rat; they'd drag each other down, their boy-curses clicking back and forth, wild things in their wild world. Back streets, industrial sites, cranes high as a steeple. Where a childhood could begin to be lost early.

His house... with a mother, a father and a cousin nobody wanted... who was Kit... was a house in a dead end by a broken wall scrawled with dirty words and names, hearts with piercing arrows and initials... A dump of a house, later he would come to realise, seriously in need of repairs which were never done. Mildew on ceilings insidiously crept spider-like down the walls when it rained; from his bed, danced a spider-jig. The narrow overgrown garden smelled rank with rubbish, weeds.

It was raining. Cats and dogs. More was coming, building up to sheet the world. Kneeling on the uneven pavement, his elbows in grey water as it sluiced the gutter, hair and face dripping wet, his nose grazed the little waves which thickened, thinned, clotted with sticks, stuff, sodden paper, engorged plastic bags. Everything was loose and blurred and he wasn't sure why he did this. With his fingers wrinkled, soaked to the skin he wasn't cold but coiled with a kind of wariness. Against what? The child he was couldn't know. Was it that he expected something to be flushed down to tell him a special message before it hurtled towards the storm water drain, then on to a stretch of river? Something was flushed down. Tapped the side of his lowered head. A furry sponge. A drowned kitten, its coat glued to jelly-soft bones, little head lolling on the broken neck. Rearing up he'd wanted to yell, but his mouth was carved from stone, his throat pinched shut. The intricacies of speech deserted him before his stone mouth melted and his teeth chattered. Like pebbles in a jar. For the first time in his eight years he had held Death in his hands and his heart froze to the wall of his chest.

Then a voice rang high and shrill in his ears; a voice from his mother in her red dress, her earrings so green they might have been green peas jiggling under an umbrella of bleached hair. His mother who looked like an angel with her shiny skin, her little potato of a nose, her sweet off-centre smile.

'Mum...?' His feet slipped on slime as he pulled up, knuckled water from his eyes. No-one there! He was alone, sealed in that wet world with the dead kitten and the rubbish; the detritus from other lives. And scalp prickling, he'd shivered with a fear he couldn't remember from before. A sudden astounding pain.

~ ~ ~

'We all live inside our own skin. And our own pain,' she says and startles him. He nods into his cupped hand, almost hearing the bristles of his beard scratch his palm. Expression sphinx-like, he recalls that during an Ottawa conference a female colleague quipped: 'Two thousand Freud look-alikes.' He winces at the vision, before her name stretches out from his mouth as if it's elastic. Not the name of the colleague, a clever enough woman but...

'Janice,' he begins with a looseness, a generosity, 'your pain; try to describe it.'

'You mean… associate?' She used the word as if pulling it free from a dictionary.

'Yes. If you wish.'

She doesn't, but twisting her fingers like fleshy wires, returns with her bitterness to the husband who decamped. 'You've heard this already but…' Early in their life together he was an in-bed-by-ten, Janice a night owl, she supported him while he qualified, her music, his gauche tastes; the fibroids, the hysterectomy.

They have the right to bore him; they pay for it… and, pious, he folds his hands, exudes interest, sincerity. He does his best with Janice, though can the dreaded Bruce be as bad as she paints him? No attempt at a cover-up, changing his stripes, to roll home at all hours stinking of perfume, then semen, once the writing was on the wall, Janice unwilling to work overtime to allow them to upgrade the apartment, relocate. The outer suburb on the southern line had suited him once. Yes, she too yearned for the house with garden; when Bruce contributed to repayments.

He's rarely judgmental, but Janice has a point. Advising is not his role but he did agree she should seek a legal opinion. Who could predict what might rain down on her otherwise?

~ ~ ~

Still the rain pelted down, fence-like. It hadn't slanted through the open door but the front windows were fogged, the inside world smelling sharp, wet.

Then his father was towering over him, wild, shaking one fist, the other clamped about sheets of paper. He was in awe of his silence. 'Dad,' he wanted to implore but locked his lips, thrust out his small soft chin. If only he'd swoop down and grab him, tickle him, even fold a bit of his cheek between his fingers, pinch. He squinted. Every shadow seemed in the wrong place:

the cane chairs, the sagging sofa, the sideboard with its freckled mirror like a gigantic egg. The radio might have been moved. No, it coughed out music, noise...

Then what he wanted was a way to escape. 'Mum...' he wailed, 'Mum...' and the big fist unclenched. Hit him. He whimpered as he fell. Above all he wished he'd stuffed the dead kitten in his pocket. Then something would be worse off than him.

'Get to your room.'

In the room he shared with Kit there was no Kit. He didn't care. But when he found Kit's marbles, he knew he'd steal Kit's cat's eye. Concentrating on where to hide it, he lifted a corner of the lino under his bed. No good, he'd disturb dust as thick as a layer of felt. In a kind of wonderment, he decided to make a hole in his pillow, twist the cat's eye in a Fantail wrapper, stuff it into the kapok. There was a huge satisfaction knowing he'd sleep on it. Maybe it would give him sweet dreams, induce a whole new planet. His planet.

He began to intone: 'My Very Elderly Mother Just Saw Uncle Ned Passing... his way to remember: Mars, Venus, Earth, Mercury, Jupiter, Saturn, Uranus, Neptune, Pluto...' He sucked his knuckles, tasted grit, and names for HIS planet sifted into his head. His choice 'Derce' which rhymed with 'purse'; incredulous years later to discover that in the ancient world 'Derce' was a fountain in Spain. Whose waters were said to be freezing cold.

~ ~ ~

'Why the hell's the water cold?

Customarily each day begins much like any other. He levers up from the king-size bed, moves around with bleary eyes, then showers. Breakfasts with his ritually cheerful wife. Well, mostly cheerful wife. Forgiving. The water's cold because one of his children adjusted the temperature, committed to her new enthusiasm regarding world resources. When it was only flushing the loos with what she labelled 'serious', he'd fought not to lose patience.

'Cold water!' He splutters, feels injured, kneads his forehead with his knuckles. Derce! 'Bloody cold enough to have come from the fountain of Derce'. And his wife who mishears 'Derce' for 'curse', dismisses this as his morning fuzziness, to assure him their daughter will soon enough value hot water at their ski lodge next month.

'Another wet day, Carl,' she murmurs, aware of his wet weather blues, if not the cause. Didn't his own analysis - compulsory for entitlement to practise - shake him up and dust him over to the admirable human being he is? Repair any inadequacies as a father? Husband?

Mid-morning he's seated opposite Roberta who's spurned the couch. He twitches his cuffs, shakes down sleeves and settling, counsels himself not to lose patience with Roberta. Roberta who is intent on banishing Robert under both physical and mental supervision to her mid-thirty needs... Robert who doubtless had a powerful left hook, threw a mighty punch. He admires her dedication. Roberta must not feel unsupported by him.

'Meanness is a game for some people,' her big knees lock together as she leans forward to 'share' with him. 'Gives 'em pleasure.'

He allows a sad sigh.

'It was at the Hero of Glebe.' This is the pub Roberta now frequents, having given up The Maid of Perth. Interesting juxtaposition. Very interesting!

'Well, that shit of an arsehole...' and, jingling the little bracelet on her large wrist, she begs his pardon, because, hungry for another life, Roberta wishes to be lady-like, though the boom of her voice swells. 'Phil, Phil Dunne, prances up, goes on and on.' Roberta shakes her long tinted hair, gives a sour chuckle. 'Cosmetics, exfoliants, discount frillies at a factory outlet for... his words: gals like you.'

Gals like you? He looks at her, more of a stare. And staring he fumbles for a memory which seems important. It evades him. But rain drums on a roof, beats through the hollows of the air. In a different order of things. Agitated, he sees it. Roberta resembles his father! Strip off the gelatinous make-up, barber away her hair, run clippers up the solid column of her neck, regrow the stubble... There's more! Fill his rooms with wafts of sausages frying in a pan of fat.

Hot and indignant Roberta is pushing clumps of language his way and now his confidence is reasserted, balloons. His skills and strategies don't often flake. 'I should see you more often. Twice a week. Shall we discuss this next session?'

Roberta stands on her long shaved legs. Smiles a child's smile, pleased.

Raw-voiced his father shouted for him to come to the kitchen. Sausages spluttered in a pan of fat. Mixed with the smell of burned toast and black-skinned bananas in an upturned saucepan lid. He sniffed. Good.

Not the customary four, but just two places were set at the table. Centred was the tomato sauce, crusted rings circling the screw-on lid. Rich Red Fountain brand! Was this a sort of omen, questioned the child he was? Like a falling star or an eclipse of the moon? And again — years ahead in the future he was to speculate whether 'Derce' ever was seen to flow with blood.

'Dad?'

His father looked at him as if he was looking for something else. Searching, as if to verify something, sweat on his forehead, his upper lip. Next he attacked his food, shovelled it in as if he was feeding something starving in himself.

'Dad?'

'Shut up and eat.'

So he ate as if he was alone in the kitchen. Skimmed a finger round the fatty rim of the plate, sucked the taste off, licked his knife.

The rain hadn't stopped.

'Dad?'

There was an oppressive silence. The air could have been hanging between them like lead. 'What?'

'Where is Mum?'

'She won't be back.'

~ ~ ~

He regards himself in the mirror, lifts his chin before he ushers in Clare. Mouths an underhand sort of smile. Clare polishes him by her attention; her beauty far from snuffed out; her voice – soft and constant – which gnaws at his ears. He can hear it when occupied with others, other things. Bruised, she tries to appear brave yet she swarms with greed. For him.

Firm, knowledgeable: 'No,' he protests... having near-to-surgically drawn forth her declaration of love. Which, weighing up the damage, she regrets at once. His face dissolves into a smile of warmth. Who loves whom? Who loves him? Sets of signs, sets of appearances, they all love him, though some – tediously stereotyped – believe it is hate.

Clare tucks her body into her own arms, squeezes her ribs in her personal fortress, then says: 'It's all a map of lies and secrets.'

'With too many maps turned to fantasies.'

'Don't we all need them? The defining key to a good life?' A chilled pause and she looks at him; no expression now, apart from the crushed expression about her eyes.

He moans and it's inaudible, rotates an ankle. A disquieting bond could develop between them. Undertones of the last taboo... incestuous love... and his head feels broken open like an egg. Last week, laughing, she asked for a photo of him. Jesus! As if sick with the burden of a secret life, he has a photo of a woman who – for an eternity – has stared out at him from the palm of his hand as his eyes bored her black and white image. To recreate the shiny skin, the little potato of a nose, the sweet off-centre smile... to tease out love. But rain or shine for forty-two years – which include the trial of his own therapy – like a man with a smudged soul, gone but everywhere, he's been unable to lay her to rest.

~ ~ ~

Kit arrived unannounced, left unannounced. With a mother. His mother. Kit's mother too! And Carl, her younger son, began to learn about the dark heart of things.

Unannounced too, his father brought someone else to share the house. Jesus. On his father's insistence, no shadow but a beacon, HE could not be overlooked.

'She didn't love you, son,' this withdrawn man who was his father told him and after the kick to his belly, his heart went hollow. 'But Jesus loves you. Always will.'

He tucked balled fists into his armpits.

'HE won't desert you' his father yelled.

He wished HE would. Prayers, prayers, prayers replaced rancorous mutterings. Grace had to be said before and after meals when the back of his neck was pinched if not bowed. With pink faces under hats, aunts he never knew existed – as well as their husbands – began to appear. His father's sisters and brothers in Jesus. Sharp-nosed and jawed, who could settle an unwelcome hand on his shoulder, then squeeze. A team of them tamed the garden to an unlovelier thing, scoured the house. Thick floury stews arrived wrapped in tinfoil which was recycled until it split, while he knew that kids from school ate in front of cartoons and soap operas; or sprawled over boxes of Kentucky Fried.

Soon, unaware he was overtaken by a profound anger and scepticism, he glowered. He didn't want to love Jesus. It had been raining - a violent downpour - and he stared at his father, daring a response out of him... agile, as he twisted free from the range of his father's fists.

Wordless, an Aunt on a mission took his arm, marched him down the hall to the bathroom, locked him in. 'I'll be back when the devil has left you.' Something left him, because he put his finger hard down his throat and sicked up the stew. Over the floor not in the lavatory bowl, so she could do her duty for Jesus.

~ ~ ~

He's told his voice is melodious. 'Till next week, Terry,' he chimes. Dismissal time; the Patek watch on his wrist dictates. He's been seeing Terry for twelve months, anticipates a further twelve. At least.

Twelve! Jesus, at twelve he was found to be bright. When in a far-from-equal world there were scholarships to be won, Terry could become super-glued in his chair. He lets a moment lapse. 'Till next week, Terry,' he repeats, startled to hear his voice thickening. Terry sighs. He sighs.

After all, to survive requires obstinacy.

MY BROTHER'S KEEPER

Rob hangs back with his shy smile before his arms go round my waist in the hug which always follows when we meet. Then, his cap slewing to one side, he beams in that sweet way of his.

We meet every Monday morning. Punctually at ten. Unless it's not possible for me, when without fail, I call his community house, make other plans for him. Yes, we're punctual at ten in the shopping mall, which glories in the name of *Rosewood*. A short walk from where he lives and safe as it's approached by traffic lights which Rob, as he stands stiffly, would not disobey. Rob's my older brother. Four years older but I've been 'big' brother from the time when, at five, I started school. If then I struggled with unexpressed resentment I can't remember it, but a few years on and it wasn't easy. Thinking back my body can tighten with shame.

Worst were the taunts, when my blood sort of thudded and words strangled in my throat, wouldn't come free. Maybe I was growing up before I finished being a kid, though this didn't dawn on me.

'Crazy,' they'd hoot. Or 'Rob...the nutter ... dumbo... away with the pixies...' The variants were numerous, Rob oblivious. Yet with a sense of pain and hurting laughter, I was stung by the unfairness of it. He had what I came to think of as his 'secret' play life to lead. Same as me – the tormentors too – lassoing and breaking in wild horses, sky acrobatics in paper-winged planes, swinging through jungles infested with boa constrictors, crocodiles.

'What's wrong with singing to yourself?' I'd bark as they baited him, and feel a strange energy steaming out of me wanting to make them understand. Maybe it was more of a head of temper at their stupidity. Didn't we all want to be *Somewhere over the Rainbow? Singing in the Rain?* Even those cruddy kids who'd fire peas from their catapults, trip Rob up, hoot and sneer? But in Rob, the butt of their jokes, there seemed no crust of bitterness to dissolve. Mine could choke me up. Who to tell? Our Mum and Dad were older than most – gentler too – and in time I came to realise they belonged to the turn-the-other-cheek school. God had given Rob into their care; many families had greater burdens than Rob who was only 'slow'. Besides they were fiercely proud of me. So when I arrived home from school messed up from fights when I got mad, I wouldn't tell them, but I guessed they guessed. Rob who was given to imitating me... standing on one leg if I stood on one leg, trying to pat head and tummy at the same time... would ball his fists, flail his arms, then muss up his hair in pantomime.

'You must not be embarrassed by Rob. Or for him,' they explained early, then explained that on occasions I would be. 'Just keep an eye out for him...' they schooled me, with the inference that they had neither the expectation nor the wish that I was to replace them, dedicate my life to my brother's welfare. 'Just keep an eye out...'

Later they made a point of telling me there would be money to provide modestly for Rob's needs.

~ ~ ~

I puff out a long sigh. Come November I'll be sixty-six, Rob approaching seventy. With his pale eyes, full head of hair, his unlined face with skin tight and rosy, time could have flowed over him. Julia's theory – Julia, my wife – is that stress-free, Rob's face doesn't record stress like the rest of us.

'Never burdened by growing up. Adulthood,' I emphasised, and we exchanged smiles, hers purse-lipped, mine amused. In this good marriage of ours with three daughters and the grief and joy they provide, Julia's concern for Rob's well-being doesn't flag.

Now in the artificial glitter and lighting that *Rosewood* spreads on either side like commercial bait for the unwary, reflected back in plate glass windows, Rob and I head for the Food Hall. Eager, he leads the way to *Coffee Country* where we'll occupy our usual table, which I hope is free. Otherwise I'll nod him towards another; Rob gets miffed if someone else fills the chairs he regards as ours. Miffed only, never aggressive; aggression one of many emotions that have slipped him by.

First things first. 'Hot chocolate or coffee?' I put to him as I do each Monday,

No deliberation: 'Hot chocolate,' he answers as always; hot chocolate his choice no matter the time of year. Then: 'For you?' He cocks his head, before he quizzes me. As usual.

'Coffee, thanks Rob.'

'Cappuccino? No? Black? No?' He runs one down-stretched palm through the air. 'Flat white?'

'Yep.'

His eyes glow with affection. 'So it's flat white for you today?'

I nod.

Having settled ourselves we stand again. Rob draws his shoulders back with purpose and, ritually, we go to the display of cakes which appear varnished behind glass. A kid licking an ice cream as canary yellow as his shirt stares; Rob squinting, then nose pointing towards a fruit-decked meringue, next the mud cake, a lemon tart, Rob settles on sticky date.

'What about you?'

I match my choice to his. I always do and this pleases him. Perhaps he experiences some sense of guidance, some sense of being in charge. I hope so.

Over the next hour – and a second cake for him – our small talk is important talk. His housemates, Phil, Mickie and Ian, his carers, Margot and Stevie. Meals, outings, television where *Home and Away* is his favourite show. Since last Monday he's been to the Botanic Gardens, next week will have a harbour trip by Rivercat... I fold hands in my lap, listen. At the table behind him, two teenage girls pull faces and I draw a shallow breath. Briefly I'm taken back more than fifty years, to a school dance when... But today I don't suspect that Rob – old/young Rob – would be the butt of their distain, with their self-absorption, their caked make-up, purple nails. And I find myself hoping that school kid in her purple party dress more than half a century ago has met her comeuppance. Flame-headed, scornful, she told Rob and the encircling crowd that he'd get a job in a nut factory any time – over all comers – while he listened with calm attention. A woman Rob's age today, if she's survived.

Then: 'Rob,' I think to ask, 'do you need anything?'

'Anything...' he repeats.

'Soap, socks? Anything?' I don't begrudge the time or money I spend on him. 'Cold weather's coming, soon be winter, need a new sweater? Like one? Maybe a cardigan?'

He looks at me, plucks at his shirt then shakes his head. 'Got plenty,' he smiles, and I remember Julia's message. She's decided to knit a scarf for Rob. Julia, whose forte is neither stitching nor knitting; who baulks at replacing buttons, so I've taken over doing that. Who has never suggested she knit a scarf for me. Or the girls.

'Julia wants to knit you a scarf. Wants to know the colour you'd like.' Rob tilts his head to one side. Blinks. 'What's it to be? What colour? Red, or brown? Green?' He lifts his shoulders. 'Blue?'

'Blue.'

'Right. But navy blue? Sky blue...?'

Rob lowers his head, stares at the table, while I compose myself to wait. Then jerking up, his voice a croak of excitement. 'Sea blue, sea blue!'

'What?'

Now his voice is singsong. On and on: 'Sea blue, sea blue, sea...'

I reach forward and rub the palms of my hands along the table edge. 'Rob! What's the trouble?'

'Sea blue,' he says again, his concentration seems snagged in the two words.

'Rob, it's just for a scarf.' But does he hear me? No, and startled, I laugh. 'R...ooob.'

If there's a hint of grievance to his voice he directs it to himself. 'Silly Rob, silly Rob.' he exchanges for, 'sea blue, sea blue.'

'You're not silly,' and if sometimes he tries my patience, with this he's creeping close.

'Sea blue,' he begins again and his face crinkles to a wreath of smiles. 'Have I ever got a surprise for you,' he now chides, imitating the hundreds of times I've put this same suggestion to him. Always it precedes something pleasant, so I reckon there's nothing to do but wait. Follow it – the surprise whatever it is – with an expression of mock wonder.

Over the years my face has been stretched with mock wonder as Rob has revealed plan after plan to me. Once memorably to buy his own car... or live in an ice-house, an igloo; the former when I stated that no way were we setting out to drive to Timbuktu, the latter during a heat wave when I was informed that Mickie planned to fry eggs on their front path.

'Have I ever got a surprise so for you,' he repeats as I lift my palms and, eyes half closed, squint at him. Unlike Rob I am aware of our surroundings in *Rosewood's* gaudy unreal shopping-world.

'Yes?'

'Almost forgot, almost forgot.'

With Rob given to forgetting, again I prepare to wait. If it's important to him he'll recover it, then like a radiator the bars will warm, the heat expand.

'Sea blue,' he says and it's followed by what is a happy sigh. 'The sea...' He quivers, opens his mouth and...' *Oh, I do like to be beside the seaside...*' Rob sings. The connection will come; loop and join up soon. 'Jool-eea, and, and...' then in a rush Rob enunciates our daughters' names, his nieces. 'We can all go and live beside the seaside... the beaut-i-ful sea...' He sways to this old tune our mother used to sing to him along with *Pack Up Your Troubles* and *London Bridge is Falling Down.*

The lump in my throat is the size of a rock.

'Jool-eea always tells me she loves to be by the sea...'

And she does: the pure blue or the corrugated steel on sombre days. The purling sound of it or the lisp as it tongues the sand, sucks back. Rob as a boy loved to wallow in water: shallow water and safe, clinging to our father's shoulders when he'd wade out, dunk him gently, breaststroke back to shore.

Now he's reaching into one of his pockets. Lips curled back, pleased he draws out a sheet of paper meticulously folded in four. He opens it, smooths it flat between us and it's a real estate flier... the blue of the sea surrounding a large brick house.

'It was put in the post with a stamp,' he explains. 'To me. Came to my letter box.'

'And...' I prompt.

'I'm set to buy.'

I know I'm supposed to pretend it's possible as I praise him for the idea. Then, expression sober, after due consideration, present reasons for – or against – which make acceptable sense to him. For it... and he'll hum with happiness. Against it... and he'll thrust out his lower lip, pout, though not for long.

He makes a tight nasal sound. 'Good idea?'

'Great idea.' And if I see the rest of his days to be halcyon days under clear skies strung together without end until his own darkness comes down, I ache for him. For us all.

Rob's eyes are on mine, puppy-like.

'Yep, it's a great idea.' I pause, adjust my tone. 'But a house by the sea costs a lot of money. Heaps. More than I can find.'

'Yep, HEAPS,' Rob picks up my word, stresses it and balances forward on his chair. 'I thought 'bout that. HEAPS. It's me who has enough money. HEAPS.' Digging now in another pocket he extrudes his bank passbook, opens it, licks over to the last entry and in triumph hands it to me.

'Think this house by the sea'll use it all up?' He bites off each word with satisfaction. 'I reckon there's plenty. HEAPS. '

Mistily I note the balance. $469.20.

'Okay?' he asks me.

It's an unanswerable question. 'Yes, okay but…' and closing my eyes, press fingers deep into the sockets. In a storm of thoughts it's like taking candy from a baby, unfairly chastising a child. Rob, of course, is not a child but here I am about to slam the door on his current fantasy.

'What you think?' His eagerness is ill concealed but, polite, he waits for what I have to say.

'Well, what I think is this…' and in his terms I explore the disadvantages of living by the sea. Separated from Phil, Mickie and Ian, the picnics Margot and Stevie arrange, no bus outings, the once-a-month-Sunday-lunch when Julia cooks a roast, and one or other of the girls come with their family. No regular Monday coffee and cake with me here at *Rosewood*…

'What you think?'

'Things would have to be rearranged,' I pull at my chin. 'Could be done, but…' Conscious that the complexities of any major re-arrangement fret Rob – always have – I feel I'm the lousiest heel ever born. Rob is frowning, and as I watch his frown deepen, my next words and actions must smooth it away. Allay all sense of disruption.

'How's about this, Rob?'

'How's about this, Rob?' He repeats, brow furrowed, his tone wavering between worry and curiosity, which I must ease.

'Come the next long weekend we'll take a cottage by the sea. All of us. Three days together then…' His lower lip trembles. 'Then it'll be back with Phil and Mickie and Ian.'

He looks at me keenly. 'Margot and Stevie too?'

'Of course,' and I see Rob's world is right again.

'But…'

But? What now? What's bothering him?

'But scouts' honour…'

'Yes.'

There's a significant pause. 'Cross-your-heart-and-spit-your-death and say that I can buy it for three days.' He touches his pass-book. 'Cause,' and elated Rob beams affection, snorts with content. 'I got HEAPS.'

GETTING THERE

S he wasn't pretty. Somehow sweetly plain.

Holly, her sister, younger by a year, was similar, has remained so... Decreed by fate, or perhaps some universal code.

Hope and Holly! Holly and Hope! Her parents, she believes, slipped up with their choice of names to ally with Harrigan, though she's known worse: Jarrah Wood, Lily Green, Thor, Goth and Vandal Stone! Later they slipped up monumentally; their mother swept off interstate by a carpet salesman, their Irish father, guardian till the end of their schooldays, swept back to the pubs of the Emerald Isle.

A slow shiver creeps over her scalp, a wild disorder threatens to press down. Grown-upness came too soon... and Hope shudders against tears. For hasn't she learned there are tears and tears?

Small children, adolescents, then young women, the Harrigan sisters were peas from the same pod: compact bodies with small feet, pale eyes, their rounded faces wide-mouthed and button-nosed, framed by hair Hope came to label 'cardboard' brown. Hair their mother routinely, and painfully, parted in straight lines, tethered with ribbons till they were nine and ten, which later led them to exotic rinses: *Titian Flame, Midnight Cocktail, Red Terror...*

Close as sisters, even if at times Holly chafed under what she considered the yoke of being younger, this ironed itself out by the time she was in high school and afforded the freedoms Hope had gained.

Hope! Just having passed her thirtieth birthday, Hope is grotesque. A misfit in a society ill-equipped to deal with her. Untutored, unwilling, a thickening in the air on being sighted, she has joined a cast of demons even though her blood pulses as it always has, marks the same beat. While Holly, with a kind of desperation offers what she's capable of offering, though both have forced themselves to recognise in their hearts – with excruciating remorse – that there's less intimacy, more unease. Which, unwatered, grows with the arrival of Holly's babies. Three to date.

~ ~ ~

Ten years ago the day was hot when Hope and Neal drove north. Like a boomerang throw the road might have been flung to hoop the coast. Bays and beaches, clean ribbed and smoothed by winds, low islands in the blues of the sea like bellied-up beached whales. Hope and Neal – in a palpable glow of happiness – Neal having just proposed. Marriage! She'd sloped her head towards his shoulder as his left hand patted her knee. How were they to know that fate – the accidental – would work against them in ten hours' time. Precisely ten. That rife with significance everything would change. A fierce white sun. Metallic rays. Cart-wheeling. A monochrome of shapes beetling over her to crash in... her world rendered black. Where she would keep on stubbornly living; to live in a place where there was no-one else for week upon week, Neal uninjured, ashen with waiting as she was cut adrift. Neal in a year to retreat from what was to become unmanageable for him. The course of their lives to crumble like cliffs into the sea.

Five more years and Hope is returned from the battleground. The battleground of reconstruction. Medical reconstruction which leaves Hope a modern miracle, yet a modern monster; her face a one-woman renaissance of the Gothic. Tapping into the collective unconscious, she details everyone's deepest fears.

Numb with misery, Hope refuses further surgery. Surgery which may improve the ruin of her face. May not. Sated by it she's unable to manage more pain, the terror of it sussurating through her head despite the many kindnesses, the many reassurances of her team… who variously, but professionally, signal in lingering ripples – yes, no, maybe – her welfare uppermost. Though there's one hungry, high-flying technocrat: Dr Whiz Bang. No! With no more talking to a hospital ceiling through dressings or tubes like vermicelli or… NO! An obscure disgust rises in her throat and hand over mouth she makes a squashing sound. However, daily warned that 'outside' she'll encounter a soulless lack of engagement to the plight of the individual, for the present she chooses to continue counselling. If not for long.

'Is that wise? Are you sure?' Holly has to agree that the efficacy of counselling is an imponderable, but she's desperate to help if she can. Her husband also, while their two younger children are not frightened when they see her. Both parents penitent, distressed, in-variably the eldest – at four – screams, and wanting to bundle him away, it's Hope who defends him, understands.

'Hope, are you sure?' Holly questions her dismissal of any future hospitalisation a second time, and as light pushes through windows, she breathes out sighs. Seems to collapse back where she sits. A symmetry of sorts to their lives when they were girls has gone.

When she's with Holly and Jim she struggles to exert a sense of suspension, hold things at bay. Keep something inside herself that can't be used up. Wishes all her clothes had deep pockets into which she could stuff both hands. Once, wasn't she, Hope, to be counted on as the reassuring sister, positive, calm?

'You sure?' Chin on wrist, elbow to knee, Holly asks again.

'Yes, I'm sure' she says, where she wants to say... How can she really know? Bring the ruin of what was a bow of a mouth to quip: while there's Hope there's life!

Holly, frightened for her she can see, is ruffled, anxious, voice tremulous. 'I'll make fresh coffee. Yes?'

'No.' Hope is learning to reject and dismiss many things, but finally not her own judgment; hard learned. Very hard learned and blood hammers in her ears as she makes her reply. 'I... I... have to try to settle to whatever passes for normality.' She blinks. A brutal normality encased in steel. She rocks forward to bring a hand down to slap the table between them. Cups rattle. 'I must,' hesitation brief, 'there's no choice.'

'Hope?'

Jim, her brother-in-law who is kind, could be a watchful referee as he puts a restraining hand to Holly's arm, knits up his face into lines. Jim, who wears heavy glasses that magnify his eyes, wants to help them both. Make certain things new.

'It's strange, making my own choices after...' a shrug, and she slides back in her chair brings knees to chest. 'After so much has been out of my hands so long.'

She sees their fixed smiles – half-smiles – of loving if pained forbearance. How can she express, let alone form the words to say that alien forces may still claim her, erode the will she needs to live on? A freak who frightens their child? A substantial phantom, no ghost? A *lusus naturae*? She sighs, feels an actual weight of melancholy. If, sometimes when they were young, Holly had an unnerving ability to read her face, guess what she was thinking, patently that time is past. And through her bit of a nose she makes a snorkelling sound.

~ ~ ~

At the window she sees the faint glimmer of the sea, watches a bird skim a bank of trees, huddles into herself thankful to be in her own flat, cradles the ring of the blind in one palm. Lime and white striped curtains, porridge-coloured carpet, two armchairs, the egg-shaped table; she's happy in these cramped rooms where, between operation after operation, she was persuaded to spend minimal time alone. Mirrors have been removed, reflective surfaces covered wherever possible. Unavoidable, though on occasions she can still catch this face of hers trapped in distorting glass.

She finds the silence balm. No streams of well-intentioned banalities. No trolleys rattling with instruments, medications, bland food. She's quite capable of cooking, shopping, though shopping is a torment. A torment because no longer must she box with shadows but the real enemy... other people. Match the way they stare with an unavailing intensity. Now she's quit the cloistered life of hospital and institutional units where she relearned to eat, masticate, enunciate, etc, etc, as well as change the map of her world, can she learn new tricks? Yes, she can; will, somehow forge a determination to get on with this awfulness that fate has flung at her.

Frozen in icy stillness, she hears herself shouting. 'Brave words, Hope.' Or are they crass? Her eyes leak and again she is overwhelmed by a temptation to run away. From her impoverished existence, a life stripped of confidence, shorn of the remotest chance of love, romance? But where?

A needling sound... the phone. 'Yes?'

'Hope? That you?'

The world, then her voice slurs. 'NEAL!'

Hope?

Oh God! She wants to shriek, though God has no place in her life. This wasn't what she was promised. Hasn't she learned there are no deals to be made... yet... from another life she feels his arms fold about her before she's forced to pull back.

'Who? Noooo.' She sucks in air, halts. Must patrol her thoughts, the web of the present; supposes she hears the caller shaking his head. And, motionless, with immense effort, joins then to now.

'It's Lance here. Jim's brother.' Lance with his wife want her for Friday dinner. With Holly and Jim. 'No kids. Say yes.'

How to protect herself? Fall into an everlasting sleep? She fixes her gaze on the floor between her feet. Disconcerted, she cannot know where she is ever welcome... and suppressing grisly emotions, in a struggle for words Hope manages: 'Are you sure?'

'Sure, we're sure,' then mock gruffness: 'Don't you dare refuse,' and in the effort to laugh she hears herself making sounds like something brittle being snapped.

'Hope?' A tremor starts up in grafted flesh under her right eye and she digs her nails into the palm of one hand. He's waiting. 'Yes.'

'Yes, you'll come?'

Where's her voice as she fights to reply? 'Yes. Thank you.'

'Good. Pick you up at seven.' He coughs. 'Okay?'

'Okay.' Neal! She frowns into an inner distance, smells long ago their times together; clasps chill arms about herself, rocks to and fro. Neal: momentarily she remains in the past, freezes the frame to remember how little they needed to say to each other to be understood. She bubbles breath, daring herself to forget before she lifts her shoulders, lets them fall. Remembering is futile and her mind thuds, becomes an ache. Taken to the edge, it's unbelievable she didn't die of the loss of him; though something was forever lost with him, and she's pinching her flesh. She cannot live in an unpeopled place, in permanent bereavement denuded of all but shadowy recollections. What then? Where? Purdah! An enclosed order of nuns! Self-imposed house arrest! Gestures of sorts, they have their appeal. No, wrenchingly, she's come to realise she must invent other plans... and thinks she frowns. Find a secret door, push it open.

At a distance there's the hum of traffic where the road runs over a low causeway. Beyond are docks, quays. Closer, in a clump of trees, birds squabble, squawk, and she bends her head to the window frame, rests it there, the sun on her face. A sun in a pellucid sky. Where under HER sky piled thick with cloud, she can't establish what's natural or best for her now... or at any time. What does she know? Half of nothing. If the future were to speak, she might block her ears, refuse to hear what it augured, what fate it may foretell.

But stripped of the naturalness of an ordinary face, will she give up, shrink into herself, stare at a grey world in stony despair? Step through a doorway to nowhere? Yes... at times, but more often quick with the sense of things... No. With stubborn resistance she'll shape out something. Strive to arrive at a destination of sorts. There is a part for her to play and that part is herself. A small life with lost highs, all-too-obvious lows.

Elbows pressed to her ribs, she interlaces cold fingers, springs them apart. Her span of existence, perhaps one day, will be purged of fear, done with blaming anyone for anything. Maybe she'll give up wearing beige!

For didn't she always – with notable lapses – above all, want to believe that we control our own destiny? Was it naïve to think we can choose the people we become? Our limitations are not only in the mind, after all. We are what we can be.

GONE BEFORE

Sam had always said: the past comes with you.

Wrong, she thinks; wrong for him. She shudders, sighs, trying to cope with a welter of sensations.

Her physical sensation is tentative. Stiff-necked, she's bent forward on the chair in the waiting room, its drab walls dotted with innocuous prints. Stage-like, a beam of sunlight from a window hits through, teeming with particles, highlights the end of a table and precisely stacked magazines.

Right now, none would cater to her tastes; she's intent on stacking up questions, then the likelihood of the struggle to get a word in edgeways when the answers begin to roll. Not just nod like a doll.

Behind the closed door there's a murmur of voices before it opens. A couple emerges: big-hipped woman, slight man. Dr Crossbach farewells them, retreats and her wait continues. Then: 'Dr Sibyl Victor?' She stands and her limbs feel loose, weightless. 'Please come in.' Is he pointedly differentiating her – Dr Sibyl Victor – from Dr Samuel Victor?

Seated again he faces her across his desk before he lifts a letter from strewn papers to peruse it while she observes his hair ruffling his skull like fur.

What's inside it? What's inside any of our skulls, but she doesn't want to think this with regard to Sam. Though isn't he the reason she's here?

'What age is he?' she's asked. 'Your husband?'

'Sixty.' So am I, she doesn't say, her feet planted side by side and though she longs to be at ease, her palms are clammy. 'Sixty in July,' and rubbing hands against her skirt, feels the knobby texture, regains composure. How could she not be agitated; Sam and his dwindling competence, his dwindling life?

'Yes.'

Yes! Most brain cells remain intact and functioning, she knows, for another twenty years. Some another thirty or more, and, polite, she waits.

Dr Crossbach pinches the bridge of his nose. 'What can I tell you?' This isn't unreasonable under the circumstances, but she's enraged. Is his expression speculative? Fraudulent? The letter he's read should inform him and she feels a nerve twitch in her cheek.

'You're an intelligent woman married to a much-respected philosopher.' It seems he's read papers written by Sam. She supposes he's not read hers; certainly not her highly praised work on the ancient philosophers: Zeno, Seneca, the Stoics.

He twirls a pencil, clicks his tongue, then responds, answers her questions. Well, at least he doesn't insult her with: 'similar to old age, Alzheimer's creeps up on you'. Forgetfulness, disorientation, an inability to perform everyday tasks. Simple everyday tasks.

She's aware there can be up to twenty percent loss of brain volume as a result of the death of cells, neurons. In the temporal, parietal and frontal lobes; that dying cells form spaces between the brain's grey matter. A fundamental function gone haywire.

If she'd hunched forwards, she holds her back straight now. 'Dr Crossbach, I made this appointment to hear the main research avenues from you. In fact, any avenue being pursued.'

He begins, continues at length and her heart stumbles, slides. Detailing, he concludes with terms which seem to slap at her; go from bad to worse. Too technical! But isn't she here for his expertise? 'Interrupting the process that causes the plaques made of amyloid-beta... cells known as amylid precursor protein... enzymes to split APP... accumulations between cerebral cortex forming plaques... dissolving the plaques to dampen their toxic effect...' He pauses, though can't know he's wearing her down.

'Yes?'

'However recent studies caution that interfering in the process could present unforeseen consequences.' He notes the lift of her eyebrows, fingers his tie. 'Interrupting gene expression.'

~ ~ ~

With leaden pace she walks to the lift. Once out of the building the sun might have been switched off. By the time she reaches the car a lashing wind is accompanied by rain... which splatters the screen as she starts the engine, sets the wipers muttering. She wants to pull away from the kerb like a madwoman who's lost all semblance of control, but of course she doesn't.

Instead she grasps the wheel, leans forehead on her wrists, and if her lips are so tight they're white, is she cursing Dr Crossbach's studied smile as he ushered her out? Uncertainty balloons. No, she's cursing his inability to change Sam.

A shiver runs through her and she's forced to look at her watch. God, it's time to collect him from Amy. Amy, his last graduate student, who has nobly volunteered as minder for a few hours once a week, Amy whose choice for her doctoral thesis is *The Peculiar Characteristics of 'Mind'*. She almost laughs, though not at Amy whom she values as a friend. Within a short distance, at Amy's terrace in Paddington, Sam is far away. Far away where she's unable to reach him, and she lifts hands, drags back her hair. Savagely. To re-hear Crossbach's modulated tones: 'Recent studies caution that interfering with the process could present unforeseen consequences'.

~ ~ ~

She flinches. Almost forty years ago, unforeseen consequences contributed to their childlessness.

Why the hell does this run through her head now? She shakes it like a dog, doesn't know whether to bark or howl. No, it's essential not to let things bend out of shape. Isn't philosophy – which has absorbed them – a manifestation of life itself? Which blossoms to self-consciousness through grades of increasing harmony? Logic, ethics, aesthetics with reference to the 'norms', or standards, of truth, virtue, beauty?

'Etc, etc…' she growls, takes a corner fast and a figure clutching an umbrella pulls back to the pavement, curses her. Shamed, she slows. God, how many assured – and tenured – voices has she heard purr with rules attributed to the Greeks, even Indian ideas of the 6th century BC. Let alone the shouting modernists. A headache starts up, gong-like drums, the afternoon reaching a deep shade of grey. Yet from Aristophanes onwards hasn't the philosopher been represented as impractical, immersed in speculations? Chimerial?

Amy opens her door with obvious relief. 'Sibyl,' she musters, smile over-bright, ushers her in, then along the narrow hallway.

'How's it been?' she asks, though there's no need.

'Okay. The kettle's on.' Amy, a pinkish person with pink complexion, somehow seems the worse for wear.

'Thanks.'

Head back, Sam dozes in a chair, knees against a low table. Here Amy has set out the simplest of jigsaw puzzles. The large wooden pieces are yellow, blue and green to slot together to make a howdah-bearing elephant.

'Is it okay?' Amy asks, and the question catches her by surprise. 'It belonged to my nephew,' and her voice, if not at the gallop, canters with a note of apology. 'There are two more and I thought...'

She pats Amy's cheek. 'Worth a try.' Does she say this to restore some kind of balance? Who knows; and with a tissue she bends to dab Sam's slack mouth, his chin. Sam? The husband who has stepped backwards out of her life.

~ ~ ~

His fingers fret at the buckle of his seatbelt, unsurprised she notes. It's rare that they cease to fret at anything within his grasp. Knives, forks, ornaments about the house, closed books which he takes to sit on his lap. Some days he just picks at his fingernails.

Seated beside her in the car she smells the smell of him: once entirely familiar, now with additions. Unsubtle additions. Her eyes well with tears and she's uncertain which of them half sobs, half sighs. Moments lodge in her memory. Assured, he's in the driving seat and having left the airport they're out in the fright of late afternoon Athens traffic. She has the map in order to navigate them via the outskirts on to the road to Delphi. 'Darling,' he quips, 'what will the Oracle – long term – have to divulge to us?'

She changes gear. Where do his memories go now he's unable to summon them? And she dashes the back of one hand over her eyes when he begins to sing. *Humpty Dumpty? London Bridge is Falling Down?* She reaches towards him and, as she pats his knee, he's knuckling into the sockets of his eyes.

'Sam?'

He blinks; again. 'Yes?'

'Are you all right?' her ever-foolish question,

He's peering at her, puzzled. 'Of course. Just thinking it's time we made our bookings – flights and accommodation – for the conference at the end of the year,' She's aghast, but he goes on. 'St. Petersburg. You've always wanted to go there: see the Winter Palace, paintings, the Amber Room, spend time at The Hermitage.' All she can do is hold the car on a steady course while traffic swarms on the road ahead. 'Kazan Cathedral, St. Peters, St. Pauls, The Admiralty. Let's have ourselves an extra week. After my paper. What d'you say?'

Gnawing her lip, she stares ahead. 'Yes, darling,' she gulps, 'Yes, let's do that. Great idea.'

'Right.' He claps then settles hands in his lap. 'I'll make the necessary calls as soon as we're home.'

Home! In the house they chose together deliriously and have occupied for so long, she's converted a room to the woolly warmth of a nursery for the former companion, the former scholar, the former man she loved. Alterations to his bathroom, she's had a stable door fixed there. Locks on its lower half so he won't wander at night. No nocturnal predator, she knows the only person he would injure would be himself. This door ensures she hears him.

But at night doesn't she try to listen beyond him? To sounds that ring the house: the lap of the harbour water, tootling ferries, murmuring trees, distant traffic hum. Sometimes she feels she'd welcome a burglar, just a petty thief, though she'd be sorry if the *Waterford* was stolen.

She could break into sobs at this. *Waterford*. Early in their marriage they spent a sabbatical in Ireland. Trinity College Dublin, and she's never forgotten a Professor Declan O'Leary. Their exhilaration as they listened to him, she had thrilled to the music of his voice as he discoursed on life, the nature of the soul, human destiny and God. 'All philosophical problems' he had stated, intimately to suggest how much he fancied her.

Someone lent them a cottage in County Waterford – flagged stone kitchen, copper pans, wild garden – halfway between Kilkenny and Tipperary. Monastic remains, relics, Norman towers, castles, a holy well. With huge extravagance at Wexford they bought their first piece of crystal. Ritually, year by year, they added another.

Thirty pieces! The significance is not lost on her. If only it was possible to trade these thirty pieces. No longer be alone with herself, invisible to him. Or convert to an ice-like theoretician, some breed of philosopher-spy. Palms to head she feels the bone of her skull. She once read that 'Memory is a house with ten thousand rooms'... so she's gone to the extreme of taking down photos of herself, then putting them in place again to try and jerk him into missing her.

He's truculent the next morning, at breakfast pushes his plate away. Mouth half open, he refuses to answer when she asks what's the matter. 'Would you rather have scrambled eggs?'

'I want, I want...'

'What do you want?' It seems only recently she checked the change in him, probed to reassure herself he was still the same. Not worse.

'I want, I want...'

This continues, she comes perilously close to shouting and the toast burns. All that matters to him is what's happening here and now. To him. Dear God, will there ever again be words between them when something important is said?

'Tell me what you want?'

'Can't remember.' His smile is edgy, then: 'Sibyl', and his diaphragm heaves.

'Yes, Sam, yes? I'm here. Tell me.'

'Can't remember,' and they're saved by Nancy. Cheerful Nancy who comes each day till midday; has done for a decade. Nancy, who handles him better than she can, cleans around him if he follows her about the house, chatters to him when he nonsensically chatters to her. After they've talked over him, coffee in hand she closes the door to escape to what has become just her study; to work at the partners' desk they'd shared. Attuned. Before his mind began to drift; a mind which is now opaque. She sighs. Against this how can they win?

Today the water is very blue. *Reckitt's Blue*, her mother would say on washday and she can only hope to exit as she did, in haste. With all her faculties. Above, the sky is stuck over with scraps of cloud. White like her father's hair in old age, so with luck she's genetically programmed to escape Sam's fate.

What the hell is she programmed for today? Idly she picks up a framed photo of him she took years ago. One of her favourites, and for the first time notes the photographer's shadow at his feet. Her shadow... and her mind becomes engaged with chance, yet she has no urge to re-run small events. What is durable, what is transient? Dear God! In the dawning astonishment of her own pain she supposes she'd made the vow 'in sickness and in health' .

It's too difficult. Rationalism deified Reason. Scepticism succeeded Empiricism, Idealism to Dualism. Pluralism, Pantheism... STOP! She will NOT become a great warm roosting bird. Cluck and cosset, care. With all that would entail. She refuses... and, head down on the desk, smells the wood and its polish... smells the warmth of their past, the sourness of today. Yes, she refuses. This is her nasty secret.

~ ~ ~

The sunset is blood-orange. When he calls to her from the deck which faces west, she's struck by the timbre, the normality of this world in which they belong.

'Darling, 'he calls, 'Sib...yl.' Her name drawn out: 'Sib...yl. Open a good bottle of red; bring out the *Waterford*.'

'What?'

'And cashews.'

She loves cashews and something inside her swells, as for a moment she can't breathe.

'Hurry up, darling. Before the sun goes.'

When he lifts both hands to take one of the glasses, it glints in the light. Lustrous, shot through by prisms of colour.

'Sam?' His eyes flicker, meet hers.

'Yes, my pet?'

'What shall we drink to?'

'Lucidity.'

Fervent, she kisses him, her lips clinging to his. Again, again. Then... Sam is scowling, black in retreat. His voice is high, hysterical, his body shakes. His head weaves from side to side. 'Who... who... are you?'

Sam!' And something ends; waves collapsing on the sand, the heavens falling. Sinking. Gone

~ ~ ~

An intolerable pressure builds in her. His voice turns papery, whines, or is blank with neutral words.

Amy, who has adored him, tells her: 'Sibyl, you can't go on like this.'

'No.' Increasingly he doesn't know her. In fact, seldom knows her, wandering lost within himself. If it's a broad world to which she belongs, under their present circumstances she, too, is at risk of stumbling into confusion, unclear of her role. Worse still when appointments – for and with him – take them out.

God above! And it flashes through her head with astonishing re-call that when students, decades ago, they – Sibyl and Sam – would walk along touching at shoulder, hip and thigh. Now he will not be guided, even led by the hand, but insists he hold her skirt between fingers and thumb. The spectacle of her thighs, her underwear, ex-posed to the general public fusses her, but not unduly. What fusses her more is being tethered; not to the six feet of a known Sam Victor but to an unpredictable stranger, who can be excited to the point of hysterics. Or spiteful, intent on tripping her up.

Yet Sam can be meek, biddable. Trot at her side, somehow with the knowledge that something is expected of him. This is worse and she boils with the unfairness of it, feels him cruelly wronged.

'Sibyl...' Amy's pink complexion flushes deeper, borders on puce.

'Yes?'

'You'll have to...'

'Yes.'

'I'll help you. Find somewhere. Vet it. And…' she reels off a string of names; friends, some already having offered to do what they can. Whatever she wants.

She nods. What she wants has been struck off the board, irretrievable. Sam was the optimist, she more the one to fall into sadness, flat.

~ ~ ~

Legs to chest, her chin grazes her kneecaps. Arrangements have been made. Today has come. Is almost over. By the open window she stares at the mute existence of land and water. Within her home, the familiar is no comfort. How to keep something inside herself that no-one can take from her?

At what was to be Sam's new home, she'd stood listening to her heart thud. Bright, airy rooms; no dark corridors, staircases, no dingy tile-cracked areas, they were shown the amenities, by what she'd researched to be a kind staff. With unnerving clarity.

Accompanied to the entrance hall by a pleasant woman with streaked hair who'd helped him unpack, Sam was docile, no tick of worry. Happy, it seemed, as he threaded his arm through the woman's arm. Listed outings on a notice board stood to their right: bus excursions, a stress-free exercise class, a visiting school choir, the *Happy Hour*. Was this last a joke?

'Dr Victor will be just fine with us,' she was told.

'Good,' she'd sort of laughed, laughter a safety valve.

Sam too had laughed, then for moments disconnected from the woman. With evident concentration he'd inclined forwards and, unflustered, proffered his hand. His intention was all too clear. She extended hers. Then, he took it, shook it, dropped it.

'Kind of you to call, Miss... err...' and something which was her heart was plummeting like a shot bird. Or a fledgling shoved out of the nest.

'Victor.' In a high warbling note it tore from her throat. 'Victor,' she repeated. 'Sibyl Victor.'

'Well,' he produced a little cough, pointed his chin at her. 'Nice to meet you. Goodbye.'

Now shadows throng around her; purple-grey like bruises. There could be a waiting stillness, and she hunches by the window, trying to convince herself she will not be condemned to misery. She'll get a grip on things. Things? Everything.

Rigid, she resists, must resist lurching... then to and fro. Will not rock.

'I need a drink,' she addresses at nothing; the nothing that surrounds her. 'Do I ever need a drink!' It has to be wrong to think she's an injured party. But given their circumstances can there ever be an uninjured party?

On the sitting room table bottles stand on an ornate silver tray once presented to Sam; a person of consequence. Among them she reaches for the neck of the whisky, then as if worked by wires, steps to the kitchen for a glass. A big tumbler in which she'll put ice. Very little ice. Heels clicking on the polished floors, she smirks at herself reflected in a mirror. Someone she should be wary of, or is she a watchful sphinx? A worn woman with sardonic eyes.

At her touch jungley music pounds from the radio. The flesh on her arms stipple with goose bumps. Then... all she wants is to use the store of herself she's held back all day. Scream, kick... 'restraint' a word never learned. Her eyes skitter sideways to the glass-fronted cupboard which holds the *Waterford*.

As if she's made of stuffing and the skin has split, she grits her teeth. To staunch the pain? No. To gather strength. A shouting laugh. And the first of the crystal glasses she reaches for is cool between her hands. Each piece, though heavier could be weightless as, demonic, she hurls it. Vengeful, flings it down. Feels her mouth working, spittle on her chin.

Bowls, platters, goblets, stemmed flutes... They sing then squeal. Shatter, slide and scatter, a myriad of jagged splinters: lemony, red and green, specks of blue. If there was a smell to them it would be rotten despite the purity of glass.

Her breath spurts, evens down to a steadier rhythm. Her blinking eyes grow still. With a cold inquisitiveness she runs her hands over the shelves, determining nothing has been overlooked. When she pats the empty shelves the fine dust could be ash.

The ash of something burned away by stealth.

TICK TOCK

Too many clocks and not enough time.

'You must come to a decision,' they say.

They? My husband John, my father, my mother-in-law, father-in-law, close and well-intentioned friends, medical and social advisers. And for the first time I am grateful my mother is no longer alive. Death doesn't wear away love, but if her voice too were allied against mine it would be even more difficult. If that is possible.

Tick tock. Fiona is twelve.

Poised on the threshold of puberty – and I look at her and time collapses the picture to the day she was born. That August night when I was afraid, fearful for all the years we would not be able to share. In a world tenanted together as I watched over her growth. Where I would guide and mother her through childhood to become a young adult, then a woman with her proper and preordained place to fill. When she would take another's hand. Utterly the same yet utterly different from my own mother's tutelage.

Was it that for the months of Fiona's gestation I dreamed in colour? Only to have the colour drain away? To a black space where it was not possible to foresee what would happen next.

Fiona: her skin is pale; between grape-white and the kernel of an almond, while her eyes have neither the blue fire of John's eyes nor the darkness of mine. Her hair is neutral but fluffy, hair that refuses to respond to brush or comb. Her lips are more beige than pink… and there's a terrible frailty to her.

John has told me that after we first heard that Fiona had been deprived of oxygen for vital minutes, my face contracted into an expression of something so complex I was unable to share with another person. Even him; which brings its own distress. A primal sweetness soured.

Tick tock. Hers was a long delivery and there was no deliverance for us. She was damaged. Not genetically, not chromosomal, but by lack of air! Enveloped in protection and protective shock, the fact that she – a milky sweet new baby – was damaged beyond repair took us months to accept. Some nights I can still dispute this when, in my subconscious, I dream of her in colour. The vibrant colours of normalcy.

Tick tock. Fiona, round–cheeked and pink as she blows out her birthday candles. When she is either one of a cast of angels in her Christmas play at school or a gum–nut fairy among the waratah and flannel flowers. Or riding helter skelter with her gang of kids on scooters or bikes.

Dreams of a different destiny.

~ ~ ~

All day the heat has been oppressive. I feel coiled in it, forehead clammy, hair hot on the back of my neck. A sparse breeze through open windows and I can see my garden flowers wilt, droop, soon to fall. Gone. How I long for evening when shadows deepen and the sun sinks and cooler air may sift through the house. Then the family of children – five of them – squealing next door will be called inside. Soon too, the grate of cicadas may fall silent… and an auditory peace of sorts will reign.

John is coming up the steps and I see his intelligent face below his receding hairline before he opens the door. With an abiding love for his daughter, he has taught himself to remain calm. He has driven Fiona to his parents for what is allocated 'Respite Care'. Tomorrow evening I'll collect her with Bear; raggedy Bear who must never be left behind. My in–laws are loving as well as good people and over the years I've had little quarrel with them. Until now. When having made serious enquiries, with our consent, understandably, in their reasoned voices, they are determined to vent their views.

Tick tock. I recognise how much I want John with me and how much I don't. It's an old feeling… like… well… like sensing myself ready for death and at the same time ready for life. Yet I've been listening for him.

I want to rescue you, his expression will say, and he wants to rescue us both.

From what? I'll query with raised eyebrows, unwilling to scan the future, though we're all too aware of the answer. We dig ourselves in deeper. Like crabs in the mud. Or is it ostriches in the sand?

He kisses the top of my head, splayed hands light on my shoulders.

Perfunctorily? NO, and briefly we face the windows, soon to be framed black wedges of night.

I don't ask the usual questions: Was she biddable, manage a smile? Or did she fuss? Did she scream? Did she notice? Notice where she was, is what I mean.

He rubs his eyes with his palms. 'Let's eat out later. Italian or Thai,' the suggestion is a good suggestion and I nod. Then nod with enthusiasm; soothed, I guess, and the least I can do.

We must try to talk about other things, can't retreat from the difficulties, panic or disown them, but slip away to some sort of safety: a cousin's second wedding unlike her first to be celebrated on a cliff top, repairs to the roof, new guttering... even plans for an unaffordable holiday. Recreational leave? Let me see; where shall we go?

Delphi, where once the Oracle spoke, pink Petra with its ancient ruins, maybe Peru where we could take that train on the precarious rails and wind up to Macchu Picchu... then lose ourselves in other riddles. Step away from the riddle of Fiona's life, ours. Or should it be more pilgrimage than travel... to compelling churches with remarkable stonework or gloomy shrines? Can it be true that plaster and paint eyes have been known to weep real tears?

'Cooler now,' he's telling me and I smile, try to gauge if this has another layer of meaning.

Tick tock. The path forks ahead. Tomorrow a meeting has been arranged with a Ms Smith and her male associate of the Guardianship Tribunal. An unmanageable reality. Subject: Fiona's sterilisation. Or not. Where mine will be the sole dissenting voice.

Ms Smith? John Doe? Everywoman, everyman? Authors of reports, regular conference participants? Dressed for the day in their serious business suits?

Dear God, can it be that – legally – there exists a possibility that Fiona could be subjected to a choice she could never understand?

~ ~ ~

'She can't manage wet pants. She's unaware', has been argued. 'How can she be expected to cope with periods?'

Fiona's paternal grandfather had looked embarrassed, hunkered down in his less open era – while her paternal grandmother, in a murmur, had offered a reply I didn't catch. Unequivocal, John stated that Fiona must not be further confused; a child soon to inhabit a woman's body. A body able to operate without the guidance of a mind – but it's impossible, we can't bypass reality.

'She must pick her way through a world that cannot explain itself – or its rules – to her. Why burden her more?' and maybe he recalls Fiona's terror once when she witnessed blood pouring from my foot when I cut it on broken glass on a beach. 'Regularity has no meaning to her; every month she'll be traumatised.' He swung his head, shrugged. 'We know there's no capacity to link it up.'

Why was I fascinated and appalled at the same time? Our world of exhausted valleys and exhausted plains with a leathery smell to the air. Yet a world where season by season seeds are still sown, bloom.

~ ~ ~

Vapour-like, something hangs over me blanketing reason and I fold my fingers into fists. Longing is a primary emotion and I haven't learned how to control it, need a clear head.

Young sufferers, I read… About 45 per cent of girls are 14 or younger and 13 per cent have not begun menstruation at the time of application.

More than half the girls and young women have some form of physical and/or sensory impairment.

Applications to the Family Court or Guardianship Tribunal for sterilisation are usually made by parents. Tears of anger slur my eyes.

Tick tock. Sweating, I've also read a report tabled by the Human Rights and Equal Opportunity Commission. Open to interpretation, I can only suppose the data is reliable, though I want a guarantee that no-one can offer me. Little is known about the long-term health effects of sterilisation performed on pre-pubescent girls. Which may cause the early onset of menopause, osteoporosis, heart disease and depression. I scrape myself together and think. Depression is accepted today, numbers among the most prevalent conditions of our world.

'Like the growth industry of Security,' I said to John, swallowing a whine that goes through me like electricity. 'Everyone scared, infected by what might never be – sealing themselves in behind intercoms, steel grilles, locks.'

He swayed on his heels, looked at me in a way I recognise and love. Then came his reply. 'She was locked away twelve years ago. No, let me finish. We both know that should she ever be abused…'

I experience a wave of nausea. It passes. Of course I know, just as I know we won't always be around – though I stay on the run with this one, lid my eyes, snap them open. Once, when Fiona was five, I made a run. For freedom. Abandoning entrapment from a shrunken world where the day-to-day living with a disabled child can never be fully enumerated, explained. Yes, I fled – as if a new beginning was possible. Led by Theseus' thread, along a yellow brick road to a street of dreams?

But my rainbow looped back, coloured by guilt, irresponsibility, fear and love. If I was separate from them by distance and hankered to be someone else, was it the truth of what I believed? Tangling with strangers and their lives, however kind, left me a stranger from mine. Empty. No safety rail.

~ ~ ~

Tick tock. Time slipping by, each passing year has been a little stick of dynamite. Explosive. The ritual order has gone astray. It's irrefutable that Fiona with a womb is more endangered than Fiona wombless. Still I hesitate. Despite the urgency.

I bleed at the thought of her pain, or is it my pain that seems unbearable? Fingers tapping, I've dreamed myself down too many paths and right now my rage is red hot, on the boil. Angry moods and I argue with John who points out contradictions. So I concede some, if few, of them, suffused by hopes – disallow a reality where there's no bargaining with this, no-one to blame.

Tonight the heat is less intense and I've turned off the fan. Lying alongside sleeping John, I heave over to see a patch of stars and the allure of fantasy is strong. I don't resist it, smile.

'What do you want to be when you grow up, Fiona?' is posed to my daughter by a genius who has a cure.

'A nurse, an actor, a baker, a candlestick maker...' Fiona responds – and my temperature takes a nose dive. Glacial, adrift in the depths of winter. Each knob of my spine is an interlaced icicle. But will I melt in the morning with the sun? To acquiescence? If so, how will it taste? How will it smell?

Tick tock. I wake up to the smell of coffee as if it's drifted in from some far-off place. Balancing two cups – his white, mine black, both with sugar – John brings them to the bedroom – John as fair a person as can be, and if everything about him is not right, it's right enough.

'Well?' he asks. The bold question.

''Well?' Are we sealing a pact?

'Well?' he asks again? And I see that living with the person you love is always, no exceptions, an on-going negotiation.

Thick-throated, I find the word, answer 'Yes.'

'Yes?'

'Yes.' And as I put lips to the cup, sip, it seems there could be a fire burning at our feet to be doused. Extinguished. Which we shall work at – and succeed.

MY LIFE IS MY TERRITORY

It took my parents years to accept me. Three to be exact, though this didn't register with me. Unique and mysterious, until my third birthday, it seemed their hopes were engaged with a higher authority, if in a rueful way. Then on a more accessible level, as if I were a riddle to be solved, I was inspected by medical specialists by the dozen, if not the gross. Next medical associates, then peripherals; though they were too enlightened to seek out toothless crones or the denizens of a nether world. Not that there weren't precedents.

Achondroplasia. As for famous dwarfs: Egyptian pharaohs used them for court attendants. Ptolemy Philadelphus even had a tutor said to be so small that he had to wear leaden weights to avoid being blown away. And on down through the ages. Why, in Rutland, England's smallest county – nine years old but eighteen inches, though proportioned in every way – a Little Person was introduced to Charles I and his queen in a pie brought to the table and promptly adopted into the service of the royal couple.

Jonathan Rupert, my name contracted to Johno. A shorter version perhaps more appropriate due to a fate which with no explanation cast me as one of the Little People. An individual well below normal size.

Short questions – long answers… long questions – short answers; with confirmation came a change. My mother pale as ivory, my father's face brick-red, his teeth a startling white, both having passed through their stages of anger, nothing would sap their strength. They were no longer baffled, even indignant. Johno's body may be stunted but wasn't he compactly made and strong? Brain functions normal, neither sawdust nor porridge between his ears. Time was to prove this child of theirs had high intelligence. So – no ashen despair. But no further children and if this was a heart-wrenching decision, I'll never know.

However, I was not raised in isolation. Our house hummed with kids, spilled over with the progeny of my parents' friends. I did not experience a diminished territorial sense as I learned to accommodate to a child's tugs and rebuffs, affections and joys.

Each morning my little feet slapped the floorboards before I clambered up and onto the vast raft of my parents' bed to be tickled, cuddled, kissed. Years before I made a connection with 'You must always value yourself' – they instructed me that dignity is to be afforded to the individual. Whoever, wherever. Though I didn't catch the full implication of this at once.

'Johno? Do you understand?'

Solemn, I'd nod my head. A large head, but mine. I wanted to please them. Though what I was unaware of then was their unlimited love. Love! Later I didn't know what to do with my grief when they died.

But at five, with one of her sweet sucking kisses on each of my cheeks, my mother began: 'Soon you'll be starting school…' and her mouth turned down. 'You're growing up too fast for me.'

Growing up, but not growing. Happy shrieks skimmed through the school gates as we entered on that auspicious morning, new cap on my head, my hand held tight. Then halted by a group of bigger boys and girls, clouds began to scud into what had been a clear sky, shadow us.

If she winced, a slow burning blush spread over my mother's face, but ever in control, she said 'This is Johno.'

'Johno...' hummed among them as they inspected me. Then: 'You mean Tom,' giggled out of a tooth-gapped mouth.

'Tom?'

'Tom Thumb?'

And if giddy with excitement for my first day at school, an anxiety took over together with a queasy tummy, watery eyes.

'Johno,' my loving and supportive mother repeated, her voice as near a growl as I'd ever heard.

'Can I be your friend?' someone asked who promptly took my other hand, so – no air of desperation – we proceeded to Kindergarten. Where, after a measuring look by the teacher at this scaled down little boy, I was seated up front.

Charged with neutrality she announced with a pursed smile: 'Johno is the same age as the rest of you. Five,' and my heart wobbled. The joys and horrors of school life had begun to kick in. It would be tedious to record, let alone recall the jibes and jokes I set off just by being me. Shaming, sad. Lacerating too, because if I'd been the butt of previous cruelty, callousness, I was unaware.

'They're stupid,' my mother declared, though, jaw set, my father had stronger sentiments: 'Ignorant. Savage. Sadistic,' he listed. Words I didn't know, but doubtless would learn. Yet sort of water off this duck's back, due to my parents' balance and the balance they taught me. 'Believe me, Johnno, they'll stop that just as soon as you laugh at them,'

My face twitched and tiger-like my father pounced on me, hoisted me high, then galloped up and down the hall before pitching me into my mother's waiting arms, the silver bangles jingling at her elbows, her eyes moist.

'Laugh at them, Johno,' they exhorted and I did, developing a funny laugh, a silly laugh, soon a nasty laugh too. A bit deeper, a bit slower; often I did my nasty laugh and if any stupid kid who continued to taunt me didn't know it was nasty, I did.

When my earliest friend, the friend who'd taken my hand at the school gate when we were five, suggested we have special – secret – names for each other, my mood darkened. Darkened with dread.

Head and shoulders bent down to mine: 'I've got the BEST for you,' and he stuck his face close.

'What?'

'Midge,' he said with a soft whistle down his nose.

'Midge?' Misery threatened to choke me. Midget! And, voiceless, was beseeching him, asking him to have a heart.

'Yep,' he grinned. 'I'll be Stink.'

Stink! Peter, who did have hot stinks about him, his feet and phew, his socks gave a giant of a whiff. His hair could smell like mud or wilted flowers, his cap like fish and his clothes like onions or chips. Stinks I liked. Not everyone though; kids holding their noses tight between finger and thumb, yelled asthmatically that he belonged in a zoo.

'Whatya think?' Peter was eyeing me.

I tried the names in my head. Midge and Stink. I felt the need of some input. Midge and Stink? 'Nooo.'

'What then?'

'Midge and Pong.'

'P…onnng…' Peter rolled it lolly-like round his mouth, tasting its rightness or not while I, smacking it in my mouth, waited. There were plenty of names for me in the playground, which were not 'Johno' but never a secret name, and I struggled to keep my voice level. 'Pong? Midge and Pong?'

A high squawk, then: 'YEP!' And out jumped my happy laugh. Next, we swore to secrecy, spat on the asphalt, two gobs cementing a friendship and a friendship with far-reaching value for me. Which led me to imagine I'd developed a sheen, an overlay to what could be a punctured thin skin.

Self-appointed Pong became my champion, taking on any kid stupid enough to ridicule or bully me. Stupid in many ways because Pong, all for justice, was not only fearless but strong. Bubbles of blood from noses or split lips proved his point – and exulting, I cheered him on, half-satisfied, half-alarmed.

Should I need a champion today Pong, a leading businessman, would prove as irresistible as a battleship. What's more, he's proud of me.

~ ~ ~

Today I'm a man in a boy's body. No freak on exhibition, no circus midget, if I suffer humiliation it's due to mistakes or misconceptions, which can bother any human in given situations, certain times. If others find my size disturbs them that's their problem, not mine. With their false convictions of the perfectibility of man. Or woman. Nonetheless, I do have a dilemma which comes with a dawning level of pain. But more of that later. Primary, secondary then tertiary education – fulfilling my parents' strongly held view of my capabilities – yes, there'd been casual cruelty. With the accident of my birth – my difference – why did I have to prove myself all the way? Faced with prejudice or downright bigotry, it was necessary to resist many a drop of poison which dripped from unthinking lips. Not that there weren't bad times but I survived. My early weapon of laughter I replaced with the weapon of a studied, enigmatic grin.

With a real life, in a real world, I graduated. No prizes or distinctions, I'm pleased to relate. Wasn't I distinct enough? I've no idea where the multitude of stories originated, but history reveals that – and I have to suppose Snow White and friends confirm it – we're not only industrious but also skilful at our work. Myths abound that we are guardians of mineral wealth and precious stones, but geology was not my choice. I could chortle at the 'Dig, dig, dig in our mines the whole day through' connotation, but indoor work in a library was where I wanted to be. Research in demographics is my field.

'If they keep you short of funds,' Pong said, 'let me know. I'm proud of you, Midge. You use your noodle, contribute to real learning. I'm just bloody shrewd.' He laughed and put an affectionate hand about my muscled shoulders. 'I'll canvas the boardrooms. Set up a grant.'

It was at Pong's second wedding that I met Linda. Pong with his: 'I'm just bloody shrewd', hadn't been shrewd with his first choice, a rapacious Barbie doll whose make-up, thick as plaster, made it difficult to detect the concrete under it. Of course, she'd not liked me.

The second wedding was quieter, solemnised at the Registry Office. We guests numbered twenty and the bride, who was diminutive, was adorable in a ridiculous hat. Feathery like a blue bird of happiness, I caught it as it swept off her head, took wings in a strong wind as they posed for the photographer on the sandstone steps. Later her cousin, Linda, diminutive too, caught the bouquet.

Following the ceremony, it was on to a five-star restaurant for lunch and as I stood about, unsure where to sit, I was placed on Linda's left. It's hard now to remember what I said when she turned from the good-looking fellow on her right to me, but annoyed with myself, I do remember thinking that I might have been a bore.

Linda: glossy auburn hair, soft eyes and a wide mouth with spaced front teeth. If this were a significant first encounter with an aura of possibilities, it didn't strike me. Yet after an exchange on the wedding couple – the roses on the tables matched to the bride's bouquet, this and that – we didn't lapse into silence. Which can happen when strangers are forced to sit side by side through a meal.

~ ~ ~

A week later Linda phoned with just a hint of breathlessness. I smiled to myself, gave myself a sort of shake and, yes, I was free the following Saturday night. She had tickets for *The Three Sisters*, and should I be interested…?'

I was. Sunny as I like to appear on the surface, Russian gloom and soulfulness has a direct appeal to me.

'Good,' she said. 'Fine.' A beat of silence before we arranged to meet at the Box Office while, biting my lip, I refused to think I may have been summonsed from the sideline when some other player dropped out.

Diminutive, as I've said, she was a head taller than my four feet five. No more, apart from her heels.

'Hi, Johno.' No tentativeness.

'Hi.' I smiled, clamped my stubby arms over my chest.

Soon we would discover that neither of us distrusted words but we used them sparingly that first night: before the lights went down, during intervals and at the play's end, when on my suggestion we drank champagne. Over the glint of glasses I suppose we inspected each other. Linda with a child-like gravity, yet somehow knowing. Me? Pleased, maybe subconsciously edging to fantasy. Neither of us seemed uneasy, looked wary, fidgeted. Later we were to confide that we could have been placing our feet on a solid path; no hovering abyss. But isn't there always an abyss?

Thoughts won't stop pirouetting in my head, a Nijinsky of thoughts, or am I going nuts? Nijinsky? More Russian soulfulness after *The Three Sisters* and their woes. But it is love not woe, swirling in ever-increasing circles which absorbs me now. Love – separate from the love I had for my parents – is perhaps a word to which I've never really reconciled.

~ ~ ~

Five months pass and every day away from Linda I want her near, with her sense of fun, her opinions, her insights, her warm scented smell. Her words with a sheen. We also share the same politics. Try as I do to pack certain thoughts away inside me, slam the door, they persist. I can't manage detachment and the weight of foreboding is heavy, indigestible.

Sunday – and we're sitting in her garden; green shrubs, green grass, and she wears green. The sun pulses down and there's the spring scent of jasmine and, feet off the ground, I pluck at the arm of the canvas chair.

'Johno…' Linda's eyes the colour of toffee melt into mine before she lifts an arm as if to shade them, scans me up and down. Her lips are compressed, but not in anger. 'I am trying to understand.'

I sigh and it's almost a laugh, close my eyes and warmth soaks through my lids till I open them.

'Johno, listen to me,' she begins with a quiet vehemence, but soon her words spill out. 'Whatever our shape we're all the same making our way through our lives' She swallows hard. 'Doubt can be self-indulgent,' a pause. 'Well, that's what I think.'

I clench fists to weapons, overtaken by the need to smash an image which has begun edging into my head. An eroding image. Me – Johno as I am – on my stunted legs, sauntering into a magic mirror. Passing through to step out tall. Tall, handsome and clean-limbed!

'Listen to me. Please. We all have rights and hopes and expectations,' then tenderly she's drawing a hand along my cheek. 'Oh, Johno, Johno. You believe you want to spare me a life with you.'

'I, I...'

'Don't you see?' She looks straight at me, intimate as ideas shift and her words with them. 'It's what I want. To be together, simple as that.'

This is beyond any dream, intoxicating, but...

'Johno, I'm not without experience. There have been relationships, a few messy affairs.' She narrows her toffee eyes. 'Big, blundering men...'

I pretend shock, but she reads me well, knows I'm not. And quirky, Linda grins to squeak at me: 'Are you a virgin, Johno?'

Grinning in turn, I examine my fingernails. 'Not a lot of experience,' I pause, 'but enough,' I tell her with just a hint of prudery, before I smile to myself.

'Tell me.'

'No.'

Now a silence between us goes on and on. And on. I hear a car hiccup, start up, rev. Outdoor sounds grow identifiable: a neighbouring hose whisking through the air, kids kicking a ball, shouting mild abuse.

Next Linda sighs and it becomes a sob. 'Johno, we're happy with each other. You do love me?'

What a question! But a larger question looms. Mountainous, unclimbable, will not recede. Hasn't this gnawed at me since puberty? A secret grief? Haven't I sought to rationalise immutable facts, live with them? I am my parent's child BUT a child of mine could favour me. If not achondroplastic – but 'normal' in the randomness of interacting genes – could I cope with that? Head spinning, mouth dry, I want to suspend everything. Blunt the brilliance of the sun.

'Johno?'

'Linda,' I plead, 'the risk?'

She thumps the air. 'Each life is a risk.'

Something flutters to the surface, my gaze falters, and I let out a laugh. Hot waves of remembrance flood through me, the dwarf. The tormenting teenagers, the gawping adults, the games of being kind to Johno, the neighbour who crossed herself at the sight of me – and I'm sulky-sullen, pout.

'Johno, Johno,' she's saying,' we all like and hate ourselves in some part.' There's no sorrowful tinge to her voice. 'I value you.' She pauses and may never know the significance of what she states next. 'You must always value yourself.'

Does the ground shake? Anything can happen, and it's with this uncanny use of my parents' words from years ago she sets me free. To return to who I am. A man who doesn't belong in a monkey house.

'Let's talk about it,' I say, breathing fast.

Soon the sun weakens, fades, garden scents intensify, sweeten the air. Dusk comes down and we move inside. Drink then eat. Arguments fire, simmer and leap again to curdle and we fall into calm. The pull of a life with Linda is strong. Like gravity.

'Johno?'

Choked up, I can tell that she guesses what I'm feeling.

'Johno?

I nod. For isn't demography my field? Bizarre. Don't I well know how the earth is peopled? All sorts. Odd, curious – and I inhale, exhale. Whatever my span of years may be, my life is my territory.

How could I resist? And why should I?

GREEDY?

Suzy's stuck in her own line of thought. Food, Food, FOOD.

'I wanna…' she shouts, tossing her head, and Ruth looks distressed. Is distressed. Distressed that as she watches her, Suzy might puff out like that awful species of toad when its tummy is stroked. Explode!

Ruth snaps the lock on the fridge. Dear heaven, please don't let her start beating with her fists – while her fingertips, steepled in agitation, graze her nose and she sniffs. Sniffs the peanut butter from the double sandwich she made no more than twenty minutes ago, when Suzy was delivered home from school. The muffin and the banana and the peeled orange and the fruit bars that followed.

Dear heaven! She'd like to believe in heaven, though not as the seat of God. Heaven she can accept as the sky: a region of atmosphere where clouds float, winds blow, birds fly. God, she feels, either doesn't exist or has deserted them. Any prayer would be a waste.

Suzy starts up again, more insistent, anything else wiped from her mind, and Ruth turns away. Longs to shut her off behind a door. Two.

'Suzy, do stop!' Her instincts fractious, she's alert to the fact that the space between them must be managed. So she kicks a path through strewn toys: plastic bucket, spades, a ginger lion, dolls with syrup-pretty faces, crumpled paper.

Out in the garden the light shimmers, while inside... 'Go and play, sweetie,' she modulates the scream of her voice. How to step back from every day? With her anguished and conflicting issues, where she'll hug her daughter to her or be tempted to slap her away!

'I wanna...' and as Suzy's nostrils flare – a little snout – Ruth chokes back her impulse to shout, strides from the kitchen to another room.

All too often my heart must be cold, she tells herself, un-mothering... and, wrists to forehead, leans back against the door she's slammed. Contemptible? She's no mouse in a bear pit, and soon, as always, will be ashamed, contrite. If only it was possible to padlock Suzy's lips over her teeth. Seal up her mouth, unseal it three times a day – but at the same time relieve the torment that plagues her child. Of course, hunger is a torment. How graphically – and regularly – this is illustrated in news pictures and pitiful television documentaries. Ruth glares. Where stomachs – bloated like beach balls – thrust out to expand between ribcages, stick legs. And she's ashamed of the phantom of a child – her child – who can appear in her dreams. If you were hungry enough, the mythical 'they' state, you'd eat grass, lick stones, choke on a fistful of earth.

Hell, she remembers when she used to diet – with no real need – and feels an involuntary pull to her middle. The grapefruit diet, the carbohydrate, the all-protein, the tomato and green pepper diet. Those Xs, Ys and Zs spruiking miracles which filled her adolescence with the unattainable; the absurdity of an x-ray skeleton and tissue-thin flesh.

'A woman cannot be too rich or too thin' was the mantra of that awful Wallace Simpson who trapped a king-in-waiting, according to both her mother and grandmother. Rounded women themselves, Ruth has adored them all her life. Her confidantes, her mentors – who have been cross as well as critical of her, chastising words to jump and flare. Yet who continue to love her unconditionally.

Does she love Suzy unconditionally? Her shoulders bow. Yes… and… no. 'No' she can't – won't – think through 'No'. Even more disloyal at times, she suspects Paul's love for Suzy is a pretence. A brush of his lips to the top of her head if she's still awake when he gets home, before he dims her Snow White lamp, as if he resents having her too defined? Ruth bows her head, shudders; does Suzy need seven guardian dwarfs? Let alone no mirror, mirror on the wall? Yet when she tucks her in last thing at night she lingers at the door suffused by tenderness.

~ ~ ~

Ruth stands staring at the vase she's filled with poppies: the reds, orange and yellows shedding glum green skins, don't want to droop, fade. But they will.

Mirrors! She moved the bevelled mirror which had hung in her room as a child to the hall. Next relocated the cedar-framed mirror from their bedroom, hers and Paul's. To where it won't reflect Suzy when she bumps herself up to lie between them like a beached and bad-tempered baby whale. Any smile a rare smile – resistant to cuddles, kisses, Paul's half-hearted engagement. Often on waking she feels desolate, and in any mirror reflected back to herself, Ruth looks worn. Is worn; her skin candle-coloured, lips pressed so hard they're white. Now, suspecting she's pregnant again – to be confirmed within a fortnight – how will Paul react?

Maybe he'll revert to singing under the shower – and it occurs to her she misses his honking baritone. There's a weight today which should be happiness but is like, like… and, savage, she kicks the pattern in the hall rug with her shoe. How to balance this? A second baby! Hadn't they both wanted one more, maybe two…?

The phone rings and Ruth exhales, feels her features set. Please, not Liza Mackay, the bossy president of Parents & Friends. The woman hasn't sighted Suzy in her first term at school, but she's been hounding Ruth. Tuckshop duty.

'Your wee girl will be dee-lighted if you can manage it. Regularly; once a week. Every child whose Mummy's a helper has a free ice-cream on Mummy's day', Ruth was informed. This enticement no enticement and a chill closed over that summer day. Radiated ice as she pictured the children tumbling out of class, last her roly-poly daughter – a pudgy balloon. Surreal. Shorter than most five-year-olds, Suzy has added four kilos to her weight since Christmas and Easter is due.

Overcome by the familiar rush of guilt, Ruth lifts the receiver, swallows to irrigate her throat which is dry like her mouth. Can she fob this woman off once more? For the third time. 'Hello.'

Any school call alarms her and her frown is wild. Is there no way to unlock the secret, subdue her daughter's constant hunger? Last year at *Jack & Jill*, the owners of the kindergarten reported that Suzy snatched food out of the hands of other children, twice was found rummaging in lunch boxes. Then, disgracefully, appallingly, scratching through the rubbish bins. Miss Gwendoline, the informant, might have had a peg on her nose.

'That you, Deb?' a voice asks and has to be convinced he has the wrong line. 'You sure?'

Of course she's sure, her voice no longer halting but flooded with relief. On his insistence she repeats her number, rocks the handset into cradle, and wonders what, if anything, fazes Deb?

Yet raw emotions re-surface and she's far from calm as she struggles through their history of intimacy to conjure up Paul. Paul: with what appears to be his growing disassociation to the problem of Suzy, while it's overwhelming her. Surrounded by their things: table, ladder-backed chairs, sofas, shelves of books, she shivers with a dim sense of where she is – who she is? Unmoored.

~ ~ ~

Anxieties bear down on her. It wasn't as if Suzy had been unable to crawl, then walk. Gibber in her baby way to form words and talk as she grew in her own labyrinth of time. Capable, she cornered all the bends in the road, yet, difficult to pin down, she wasn't quite like the children of friends. Other children. Ruth wants to annihilate details.

With Paul, they tried to hide their ignorance and fear behind the *clichés*: all in good time, when she's ready, tomorrow will take care of itself... But in an unforgiving glare of light, huddled together like conspirators it became difficult to persuade themselves that all was as it should be with their daughter; her arrival their personal miracle. Which began to crimp at the edges, crumble. What to do? Neither of them spineless, but how to take a stand, let alone ferret out answers?

Ruth flattens her hands on her stomach, holds them there and dropping into a low chair, drifts back. Five years. When Suzy entered the world, wanted and loved to the point of idiocy. Perhaps they were too happy? Adorable to her parents, she was underweight. Medical terms translated to the fact that she was born with weak muscle tone; their sole cloud. 'No cause for alarm,' they were told in a low-ceilinged room, the expressions on professional faces implying: No big deal. 'However, she needs to be force-fed.' A pause. 'Disappointing, time-consuming, but manageable,' smile after smile confirmed. And Ruth was weak with relief, remembers weeping.

~ ~ ~

Things changed. Suzy began to eat. And eat… her baby face dominated by a fish mouth. Forever open. Grumpy, never happy, never satisfied, the rage of her infant tantrums seemed to exceed Ruth's experience of rage. With bowls scraped, emptied, the small face was an exploding grenade when nothing more was offered. The shrapnel could have lacerated Ruth, wounding her with her inadequacy to assuage her child's hunger. Pap in the form of porridge, puddings, pulped fruit graduated to solids which were never solid enough. With no idea what to do, devoted, Ruth did the obvious. Prepared more food – but this was no recipe for love – while in each other she and Paul noted flesh that wasn't there. To become nervous, then afraid.

Suzy's eyes seemed forever to slide in search of food as she sucked or gnawed her knuckles. Scowls pleating the little brow, from her high chair her downy head continued to incline to fridge or stove. Sticky-fingered, moon-faced, jam or juice on her chin, often wretched, Ruth feared she wanted to strangle her. Ruth who did not believe she could hurt a child, struggling not to think of it.

Loss of control is not comforting. Her mother and her grandmother disagreed. A firm slap had never harmed her, and united, they soothed Suzy's mother. Suzy too, must learn there are unavoidable limitations in life. Greed was one. Warm-voiced and indulgent, they joked as they heaved her about. 'No one wants to roll you away on outsize wheels' or 'Boil you down in a big saucepan!' they would nuzzle her over-chubby cheeks, tickle her over-round tummy when the clothes they enjoyed buying for her did not fit. 'Pack them away for Number Two,' was said.

Unsaid: how will she be when she's older? Shape? Personality? While Paul's response was resignation mingled with something more. Resentment?

Advice came from all quarters, but Ruth sought more – felt she was bent on an Indian rope trick, hauling herself up, slithering down. While the *clichés* bubbled to the surface like comfort food: 'She'll grow out of it. Puppy fat. Better than skin and bone.'

Really? And wraith-like Wallace Simpson tottered out of a narrow grave.

~ ~ ~

Insistent rattles and bangs penetrate these thoughts. Disinclined, Ruth shakes her brain awake to alert, listens for the chain on the fridge, before all is quiet. No! Did she leave the bread within reach on the table? Was Suzy tearing at it? Ramming hunks into her mouth? Columns of ants carrying off the crumbs?

Bing, bong. The clock behind her strikes and she counts. Four, five... and Ruth's head angles back towards the kitchen. She sighs, now seems to sigh over everything. Should she drag the bread away from Suzy, then prepare dinner?

Six o'clock – and Suzy is sulky, fat little paw clenching the spoon as she ladles more to her mouth. Her lips glisten – and thickly, through spaghetti, she's demanding: 'More. MORE'

'No.' Don't think, Ruth counsels herself as she swivels away, straining for a gentle tone. 'We must leave enough for Mummy and Daddy later...'

'Why?' Tub-shaped, Suzy's jaw snaps on air. 'I wanna...' she flaps and shrieks.

'NO.' Aware of the power a mother holds over a child of five, wrapped in dismay, does she want it?

She expects Paul will be late. He is – and mouthing a greeting as he comes through the door, Ruth won't inquire why, does not want her face a reproach. His touch sweeps down the braid she's made of her hair, then jacket off, yanking loose his tie, he grins at her. She blinks.

'I need a drink,' he amends to: 'we need a drink.'

Glass half raised, she's aching to give him her news. Does not want to be distanced from him.

'I've some news,' he says. 'Something which might...'

'Might?' Doubts worm through her imagination, and gripping the glass is aware that, like her, it's far from shatterproof.

'Yes. Might.'

Paul?' She queries and although it's not cold her teeth start to chatter.

'No. Just listen.' Breathing erratically, he drains his glass before pulling a folded sheet of paper from his pocket, smooths it flat. He has large hands. 'I came across this just last week.' She makes to interrupt. 'I needed it verified before I told you.'

Body taut, her fingers lift, encircle her throat. It would appear that nothing's solid, nothing's fixed. This man she loves has his secrets too.

'Listen. Listen.' he repeats. 'This really matters,' and Paul's voice begins to roll through words. 'There is a condition known as P.W.S...'

'What?'

'PWS,' sonorous, he's emphasising: 'Prader-Willi Syndrome,' and he begins; 'The most common genetic cause of obesity that is known, which can affect about one person in 15,000. Those who suffer from the disorder have no control of their appetite.'

She can't hold back. 'Then it's more than greed? Gluttony?'

Jaw set, he leans forward and with his free hand gives a thumbs up.

'Paul?'

'Ruth, listen. They must have their food limited. Plus a strict exercise regime in order to control their weight.'

Her teeth bite her lip, she's scanning his face and right now it's a map she's not certain she wants to read.

'Between the ages of two and five children with PWS may begin to gain excessive weight and develop an obsession with food which can be life threatening.' A pause. 'Their metabolism is depressed, making it difficult to rid the body of fat quickly enough.' He raises eyes to hers. 'A mild intellectual disability and poor co-ordination is also common.'

She swallows the impulse to interrupt, to sniff and smell something now that could be a garden gone to seed – her hopes rising or falling as time ticks away?

'Children may be placed on hormone programs to counter stunted growth, another sign of the condition, and most require care throughout their lives.'

Desperate to absorb this, the muscles in her face stiffen. 'It's incurable?'

'Listen. Please,' and nodding her readiness, their mutual bafflement begins to recede as he prepares to go on, does go on.

'PWS is not an inherited disorder, but an abnormality of chromosome number 15, which occurs at the time of conception.' Imperceptible – but she knows him well and catches it – there's a change to his tone and she's near to panting as she waits. In this light his lips look grey. 'I... I... discovered... that in about 70 percent of cases the absence of genetic information from the father results in this abnormality.'

Ruth sucks in her cheeks, reels. It is not the fault of a God she can't believe in. It's his! Now he's taking her glass and if it's his intention to take her hands in replacement, she tucks them into the hollows under her arms, squeezes herself.

'I've contacted a cytogeneticist. At the Children's Hospital...'

'What!' She gawps at him before her head drops and her hair falls over her face. Seconds later, she's very angry, unhinged, floating without an identity, nudging insane. Was he, Suzy's father, about to put Suzy on public exhibition? Suzy a freak? Or lead her in and out through how many doors of clinical detachments?

'Paul!'

'Hold it, Ruth.' One rigid palm flies upright. 'While tests have been available for twenty years, clinics are still diagnosing the condition in adults.' Now his purpose strengthens and he's relating what he himself heard from a voice of authority.

'Suzy?' Eyes hooded, Suzy's mother flops onto the sofa. 'It's been recorded that these kids can be unhappy. What's more, never satisfied.' Pulses of sweat break out above his lip, and somehow he looks very young. 'We've an appointment...'

Behind Ruth's eyes, tears burn. This leaves her gulping and in such confusion, she could be a stranger to herself.

In the silence between them Paul gives a sort of laugh before he strides the dividing steps to her, hoists her to her feet – rubs his hands up and down the chill of her arms.

'Paul...'

'We can grapple with this,' he says, and if the atmosphere had grown heavy, it begins to ease. No longer insupportable.

We can grapple with this! Yes. She straightens her head, widens her nostrils. What does she smell? The certainty of him – and for the first time she acknowledges the smudges under his eyes, the lines creasing the grainy skin of his face – and again, he's become readable to her.

'Ruth?' Her name sounds husky but as her brain locks on this, she's comforted, aware that they could be nudging through to a kind of safety. A grey world may not have been rescued to peacock colours but...

'Paul,' her fingers lift, to close about his wrist. Isn't every child's anchor parental love? She should never have doubted Paul. It has not slipped him by. So a kind of waiting is over and all that will follow has begun.

WOBBLY TRUTHS

Edmund House. Built 1906, it's a house that insists on being lived in. Though by no present member of the Edmund family.

There's a fat sun today which earlier slanted in to wake four of the twelve residents: Rachel and Felicity who – amicably enough – share a room, Jack and Guy located further down the hall. Of the four Rachel is given to nightmares and when her bare feet slap along the corridors as she seeks comfort in the familiar shapes of rooms, she's relieved to encounter Jack. Jack... who's driven to rinse his hands at intervals which immutably seem to be set by a timepiece in his head.

Donated to the Department of Health, in accordance with the expressed wish of a generous benefactor, Henry Wansell Edmund, this once-imposing mansion has been legally chartered – under watchful Trusts and Boards – to house individuals with an inability to house themselves. No exclusive occupancy by specific religions, specific diseases, gender or age... notwithstanding the odd hiccup, this is a supervised community, able in part to move within the broader population. A sanctuary, never a prison.

Today, while at a short distance a haze hovers over the sea and the seaside suburb, redbrick Edmund House glows in its tight garden dominated by a magnolia grande flora, larger grounds sold off, nibbled away. Heavy creepers swarm over an outer building which once garaged Edmund motors, an attic flat above for Edmund chauffeurs... now out of bounds.

Eight in the morning and a radio blasts from the kitchen. A strident mid-chart pop, – rah de rah deee – and when the kitchen door is flung open, birds begin their to-do over stale bread scattered for them on the path. Soon there's a commotion in the house. A good commotion as the residents clatter down the stairs to the dining area under its high, ornate ceiling... and breakfast. Homely sounds follow: chairs scrape into tables, spoons scrape bowls, knives, forks are occupied with eggs, baked beans, squares of toast. When brown pots gurgle tea into mugs, voices demand: 'Give us the sugar, the milk' and if something drops, someone yells.

For the last months Felicity and Rachel, Jack and Guy – following neither pre-arrangement nor discussion – have chosen to sit together for meals. Territorial seats are rarely questioned though a fight might have broken out if Mrs Carmody – no stranger to discretion – had not with exhaustive patience directed a would-be interloper to the window table. Here he gives a running commentary on clouds.

Felicity, Rachel, Jack and Guy? Who together have set up some new version of their lives. No conscious plan or certainty, just re-moulded themselves. Grown into one another.

Felicity? Often just watching the shape of things, she can be remote from the others but they're her friends. Awkward, ginger-headed, milky-skinned, she's thin, too thin. Though when she remembers to eat she eats as much as anyone else. Her expression frequently unreadable, given to staring through an immensity of space. If the others fail to see what she sees it makes no difference to them.

Rachel? Heavy-lidded, an Eastern tinge to her looks she has stark black hair, stark black eyebrows. Small-boned, she's not thin. Tubby, she likes to wear gaudy stuff, floaty stuff, favouring oranges, reds, mauves.

Guy? Given to working methodically at the food on his plate, he's cheerful. Big-bottomed, he laughs a lot as he waddles about in his many-pocketed shorts. Oiled tufts of hair are flattened to his head. The oldest of the foursome, Guy takes most things at his pace, forever calling 'Wait for me!' And they wait… because if hurried something inside him can convert to a pounding machine. Which might shatter, or worse, scatter him to kingdom come. Whatever the season Guy wears open sandals, on occasions pulls on black socks.

Jack? In contrast tall, wispy, stooped, with his impassive gaze, smooth-faced, close up he can look as if set behind an invisible shell of glass. He's owl-eyed, blinks a lot and for Jack nothing is as it was before. No more wailing like a calf, here he's safe, the world no longer a wound that won't heal.

Today is special – no sheltered workshop – and Mrs Carmody joins them. A small woman with a large heart, staggeringly kind… little slips by her concerning the welfare of her charges.

'Well,' she says – her morning greeting – before she adjusts half-smoked glasses to the bridge of her nose. 'You've a busy day ahead, which should be fun.'

She holds a pencil to her front teeth.

'Fun, yep fun.' Rachel beams, red scarf jaunty on her head, to infect Guy who grins too. Next Jack, while Felicity lifts her hands from her sides, shakes them against the yellow roses of her circular skirt.

'Good.' From her jotted notes Mrs Carmody reminds them that she'd like them to buy (1) a new toothbrush for Jack, (2) sunscreen for Felicity and (3) a book of stamps at the post office for her. They're also to have lunch at McDonald's, be sure to keep their bus passes safe in pocket or handbag and... spend their money carefully.

'Each of you has $20.' She pats the table, circles a knot-hole in the wood.

Guy tips his chin out, is concerned, understands but... 'What if...' his breath audible like a child's who must concentrate. 'What if I don't want nothing but lunch?'

'That's fine, Guy,' but she visualises a hamburger high in saturated fats, chips and a chocolatey pudding leaving little change as Guy jumps up, gives a succession of awkward hops. Endearing Guy, in the main obedient, but given to an unnerving playfulness.

Turn by turn she regards them. 'And, tell me, what is VERY important?' She taps fingers of each hand to her head then adds 'Think.'

'Thinking, Mrs C... thinking...' from Rachel, but among the erratic clatter that surrounds them they present a waiting quiet before they tick through what they know – the bus stop at the corner, the terminus where they always dismount. Yes, to be back here, returned to Edmund House well before dark.

'What else?' That they take nothing out of a shop before they pay.

It seems something flexes the length of Felicity's spine. Through washed-blue eyes, twisting her hanky, she stares levelly at Mrs Carmody, to hesitate before in a dreamy thoughtfulness she's saying: 'We must stick together...'

'Yes?'

'No matter what.'

Wordless, Jack mouths: 'No matter what'. Again. 'AND', energetically from Rachel, 'we got our rights.'

'Yes,' Mrs Carmody agrees. 'You've got your rights.'

~ ~ ~

They're bunched at the bus stop in part shade from a plane tree, porky shrubs. Guy twisting one sandalled toe into the roots, Rachel's hand in Jack's while Felicity, uncurious about wherever they're going, could – or not – be watching out for the bus. The 509.

'You're late,' Jack squeaks at the driver who is familiar with 'The Edmunds' as he calls them, a man of warm and encouraging nods.

'Sorry, mate.'

This matters to Jack, makes him tearful, a bit blubbery, and Rachel's arm grips his waist, urges him up the step. Then next – sticking together – down the aisle. Though not before her lips go tight, her bit of lipstick striates and she chastises the man at the wheel.

'You shouldn't do this, you know. Keep Jack waiting. Us neither.'

'Sorry, luv,' he revs the engine, 'but I'm doing my best...' and she's placated; further placated when a blonde with big red mouth and pink-framed glasses gives her a wink.

In single file they shuffle to the back then, lowering themselves to the seat that holds four, they jounce along in the certainty that they're on their way. With no risk of being carried beyond their destination, the 509 terminates at the big shopping mall.

'Might just see you on the return trip, mate,' the driver addresses Jack, whose Adams-apple bobs like a cork in the long bottle of his throat, Jack to astound him by pecking a kiss on his cheek.

With the wonder of a little girl discovering a stockpile of sweets, her cheeks flushed, Rachel is first at the automatic doors which glide open and reveal a delicious world of reds and oranges and mauves bulked out by the rest of the rainbow, skeined by thudding beats of sounds from speakers which not only provide music but exhort the public to buy, buy, buy. Bargains, sales, reductions galore. Great value, special value, fantastic value... little of which makes much sense together with the puzzles of logos, names. Caught up in the fantasy of a dream, she's bug-eyed at everything red, orange or mauve, sleeks her tummy, her rounded hips.

'Come on,' she shouts to Felicity and Jack who are linked by hand and mean to stay that way. At least till they acclimatise to these sights, sounds, inviting smells, the light now neon-streaked.

'Wait for me...' and it's smell that tugs Guy forward... to a popcorn machine, the air about him percolating with a sweet toastiness. Licking lips he waits his turn and, captivated, watches as the corn leaps and surges in its plastic barrel. He thinks it reminds him of something else. Something... but can't remember what. What he does remember is Mrs C telling them to spend their money carefully. So carefully, in a wash of relief, he extracts his $20 note; lays it on one flattened palm, carefully smooths it twice.

'Large or medium?' This from a woman with chipped front teeth wearing a forage cap behind the counter.

Guy doesn't know but it's Jack who replies 'Large.'

'Okey dokey, luv,' and Guy proffers his $20, open-mouthed to be given three notes in the exchange, fifty-cent pieces. Goggling, he stows them away, his hands two open spades, to receive the popcorn.

'She give me more money. Lots,' he splutters between a mouthful before in his kind of ceremony he offers the brimming carton to the others.

'That's right,' sage Rachel informs him. Rachel with a skill for small numbers is savvy with regard to change. Happy in the task, she's their appointed money person with Felicity aware, though unconcerned, and Jack far from astute with dollar notes and coins. Having long since coached herself in the need to appear very calm, Mrs Carmody would not have her pressured, but over weeks last year, painstakingly, Rachel was taught to use an ATM at a bank. But this had to come to a stop when in one day she emptied her account. She wanted a nose-stud, a diamond, not just a bit of coloured glass.

'Who's for a drink?' Me, me, me, me… and with Coke for Felicity, chocolate milk for Jack, orange cordial for Rachel, a lurid fizzy lime for Guy, they cast about for a vacant table in the Food Hall.

'Oooh…' Jack drops his chocolate milk but with luck the carton doesn't split and he bends down to recover it. Then – 'Ooooh…' It's a stricken infant's cry as a canvas boot tumbles him over to spread-eagle on the floor.

Popcorn and fizzy lime at a precarious angle, Guy hunkers down beside him, Felicity retrieves the chocolate milk to sidle round at nasty laughter from a big kid in black jeans, T-shirt. But the laughter is abrupt… and brief.

'You kicked Jack in the bum!' and Rachel charges. Next she's kneeing him where it hurts with the accuracy of a girl trained in self-defence. Plus invective. 'You sodding little shit,' she tilts up her chin which brings her in line with his chest, then to a gathering crowd she lets fly. 'If you think we're a pack of galahs, you just oughta think again.'

Nondescript and dressed in dull browns, a woman steps forward, claims the bully then spits out... and it's savage – 'THEY should never be let out.'

'What you mean?' This from Guy, his mouth working, slippery with spit.

Under the protection of his mother the big boy dares 'Ya babble, ya baboons.'

'Babble!' Rachel is outraged. 'We don't babble, we talk,' and she sniffs. 'Same as you,' then, a fussy duenna, she proceeds to gather together Felicity, Guy and Jack. But where is Jack? 'Jack...' her body taut, her voice is plaintive. In response a girl with ridiculous hair, which at once Rachel appreciates is orange, points ahead towards a sports store, a shoe store, a book store which lead on to clothing store after clothing store where, with massive will power, she refuses to let herself halt by a pouting plastic model draped in mauve spangled top, second-skin jeans at the entrance to *Girlie Things*.

'Come on.' Felicity with a look of knowingness, appears to be listening to sounds beyond her range, but has the presence of mind to tug at Guy to prevent him bumping off to the right.

Centred under a high dome and ringed about at floor level by a low artificial hedge, a fountain plashes. Water falls from a construction of glittering signs of the Zodiac: Leo snarls water, Taurus snorts from stretched nostrils, Cancer sprinkles, while in twin delight Gemini spouts...

'Jack,' Rachel, Guy and Felicity breathe as one to the whorls of hair at the back of his head and, brimmingly relieved, they prepare to wait. Jack – for the moment – is where he wants to be.

'Best get your friend back here over the greenery before Security spots him,' someone warns, and clamouring to join Jack, a toddler in pink with stumpy legs like rolling pins is strapped into a stroller.

'What's Security?' Guy asks.

With queenly conviction Rachel answers that Security is a friend… like Mrs C but not as good… while in some sealed chamber of her own Felicity either dreams or broods, lets her eyelids flicker before she sucks at strands of her hair.

All in good time – Jack's time – he levers up from his knees to trawl both hands the length of his khaki pants. Then, breathing in satisfied puffs, a fullness in his chest, he rejoins them to link arms between Rachel and Guy. But Guy stiffens, glares, withdraws his arm before: 'Wait for me…' then, impetuous, trots to link up again.

'Where's *McDonald's?*' he asks, but it's Felicity who reminds them they should buy toothbrush and sun screen before their money evaporates. The post office with Mrs C's stamps can wait. Because… letters have to be written first and maybe she's not had the time.

A pharmacy is located and it's Guy who declares they should inspect all the toothbrushes – brands, colour, shape – before Jack is set to purchase his choice. Jack chooses an *Oral B* medium, handle blue.

Thrusting out her skinny neck Felicity is unwilling to be confused by shelf upon shelf of sun screens, reaches for the nearest and takes it to the counter. But here, with a shake of the head, the pharmacist directs an assistant to find a product more appropriate to her skin type: *Sportblock, Sunsense low irritant, Quadblock 30+.* Decision made, Felicity nods, face hidden behind the fall of her hair as she ripples back the zip of her teddy-bear purse, parts with $7, Jack excavates a pocket for his money while Rachel shifts from hip to hip beside him. Guy stands by.

The pharmacist, who has a sunny face above his thick-veined neck, slides four packets of barley sugar out of a display fixture, places them alongside the bespoke sunscreen and toothbrush.

Half formed words buzz on three tongues, but Rachel's their spokesman. 'We didn't ask for them,' and with a sharp finger points to the four additional packets. She's come to understand that there's always a need to have someone in charge against unplanned eventualities. She sees Jack and Guy's eyes lingering on the sweets. 'Not that we can't pay.' She ramps up her words: 'You can ask Mrs C...'

'No need for that. Okay? It's like this...' behind his counter the chemist lifts his greying eyebrows, begins.

Rachel has her statement ready, ramps up the words. 'We've got rights, you know. Our rights. We can pay,' and her voice is about to thicken with distress. 'We...'

'Of course you have rights.' He pinches the bridge of his nose. 'I know that, girlie, but...'

'But what?'

His hesitation brief: 'Today with every purchase...' and Felicity nudges Rachel to whisper: 'Bargains galore. Specials.'

Rachel is unconvinced. This feels wrong. Besides, isn't she good at numbers? 'We only want to buy TWO things and,' she counts, 'there's FOUR more and... that makes SIX.' She faces a benign smile.

'In my shop it's how much things cost, not how many,' he insists.

'Well... If that's right...'

'That's right.'

'You not cheating us?'

'No.'

'Okay,' she casts a pretend-frown at him, turns to the others, raises her chin. 'Okay you guys?

They nod, Jack laughs a high whinny and all but Felicity laugh with him, Guy twisting the wrapper off his barley sugar as they leave.

~ ~ ~

McDonald's presents few problems. Taken there twice by Mrs C and again by a volunteer with a saucer-sized V for Volunteer badge pinned on a pink lapel – they weave through a crowd of shoppers, baby carriages, towards the Food Hall. It's time to eat. *Mcburgers, Mcfries, Mcsundaes,* three of them choosing caramel sauce, Rachel raspberry. But problems lie in wait.

Guy, knees open, is beside Rachel who snaps every mouthful shut on the meal. Causes and consequences seem out of Jack's time, his gaze steady ahead on Felicity whose eating, swallow by swallow, is prolonged. Unfolding herself to stand when she finishes, Guy takes her wrist in the warm pad of his hand to guide her through the maze of tables and out.

To ambush! It happens fast. Louts on skateboards – six of them – spiked gelled hair and menacing belts studded with silver bullets reel past them, circle back, again. Again. Slitted eyes glide over the quartet; malignant eyes, and one acned face presses up to Rachel's, who, fingers splayed, holds her head as her red scarf slips a bit.

'You, you…' Jack's voice trebles up. His cheeks begin to work like pumps… in out, in out… as if they can't stop. Watching him, menacing him, waiting to see what he'll do, the gang edges closer to Jack. Then galvanise as one force to shoulder Jack. High-stepping… stealthy, prowling… they feint and dodge, retreat, snigger, again advance. With the possibility of thrown punches, attack, silence radiates from Jack like heat. He wants to be a hero but doesn't know how.

Suddenly, surly as an actress upstaged, Rachel snarls. 'Get the hell away from us,' and an old man with skin like elephant hide strides into the scene.

'Get the hell away from them, you hear me.' It's a smoke-roughened voice.

'Yeah, yeah, Granddad,' and his towelling hat is flipped forward from behind.

'You kids okay?' he asks with the right to call them 'kids' from his many years, before, with a contemptuous gesture, he shades eyes against lurid lights and flickering neons, to assure himself that the gang, hooting back at him, is about to disappear into further reaches of the mall.

Guy wears a queasy grin, while head down Felicity's narrow shoulders shake. Rachel could be in the grip of jittery excitement, her breath jagged on loose lips.

'Okay yes, okay,' this from Jack ... who reaches out but not quite touches the weathered hand.

Bunched shoppers are inquisitive, watch. Others swivel away, expressions emptied out, retreat. 'Poor souls,' someone states.

If The Edmunds were listening they'd hear tongues click and murmured comments as if they were branded exhibits of some foreign kind. They've experienced this before, and openly facing these onlookers, Rachel now turns an outraged backside... gives her whistle of command. Somewhere, sometime, in shadowy dream she recalls a man... a wiry cattleman with river-stone eyes and flattened nose, capable, affectionate, working his dogs. It's a dream that can comfort her.

The tension of menace is quick to fade. At the *Fruit Emporium* massively piled with produce, Felicity buys a pear, snaps her teeth into it. Mouthing in silence as she chews, Guy is reminded he'd sure like to eat again. Savouring choice, he hovers over a punnet with strawberries big as plums. But next door, strawberry gelato beckons in a sugared cone.

'Strawberry,' and he butts his head to point as Rachel goggles at the array of vivid colours. Gee, and she's grinning as she reminds herself she's set on seeking out just the right shop where she's also set on buying something special for herself. Yep. She's going to be very choosey; won't be hurried. And this time will not be told by any bossy shop girl what suits her. Or what does not. As well she will not forget her copy of *Dolly* from the news stand.

'Well?' Scoop in hand the gelato fellow gives a shrug, waits on their choices, nods and digs into the vats. Guy is sure he could eat the lot, and in a far from tentative tone, bold now, Jack states: 'Give him a full scoop,' and to their surprise Guy gets a scoop and a half.

'Ta...' Guy thanks him, satisfied, and they meander on towards a catwalk strutting out like a toy jetty from a bikini store.

'First to view,' they're informed by a sleek female commentator with her ice-cream sized mike, will be Sharonlee wearing *Sand & Sun*,' a breathy pause, 'followed by Jade wearing *Hotspot* '... and no warning... feverish, Guy's blood swarms to the surface of his skin. Clutching his strawberry gelato by the cone and abstracted, licking as it melts, he focuses on Sharonlee. He'd sure give a million to be licking her; though doesn't attempt to figure out a million of what. Everything about her could have been made in miniature, looks sweet: small feet, small hands, small tits. Yum... and his penis swells in his shorts, stiffens... could be the size of a flesh-covered rolling pin.

Goggle-eyed in alienation, words he'd like to use strangle in his throat. Her baby sandals click like castanets and there's more. Sharonlee is within touching distance and she heaves a fluttery little sigh. For him, Guy. Then it's Jade wearing *Hotspot* and his breath's like a rackety engine as Jade pouts her pink flower of a mouth. At him.

Next a musky perfume cloys the air, Cindy wearing *Golden Scales* appears, a lei of frangipani strung round her neck and glittery scraps which means she'll get baked red all over at the beach. Today Felicity bought sunscreen and…

On the point of loping away to the pharmacy to buy sunscreen for Cindy, his fidgety hands tap his thigh, his genitals… his shorts sticky now with melted gelato. And if the tips of his ears sizzle like fire, his underpants warm, gluey, wet, Cindy sure would thank him for his willing help against sunburn on her snow-white skin.

What if the barley sugar man has closed shop, gone home? What if instead some great grump now stands resolute as a rock behind the barrier of the cash desk looking to serve everyone except him. His teeth sink into his lip. No; Cindy will have to do her sun-baking in the shade.

'And here we have Dolores wearing *Dolphin*…'

The heaving sigh like a knife drawn from its sheath is his… and Felicity pokes him hard in the back to indicate they're off.

Uncertain what's real, what's not, among these many known strangers – and the girls – back at Edmund House he might just ask Mrs C to have Cindy and Dolores and what's-her-name, come over. Come over for a ping-pong night. He doesn't doubt Mrs C will think it over; hand to chin she thinks over heaps… Besides everyone knows Jack's good at ping-pong. His features squeeze up with pleasure. Whoopee, ping-pong. Isn't Cindy and the rest of them some great idea!

~ ~ ~

At length after Rachel examines at least a dozen trendy tees, then chooses an orange tank top with mauve sequin stars, packaged for her in a tulip-flowered carrier bag. She persuades Felicity to choose a beaded bracelet with a gold clasp.

'Real gold?' she asks an assistant's raised black-pencilled eyebrows, parted crimson lips, as she proffers Felicity's $4 and receives back a 50 cent piece.

'Real gold,' the deadpan reply, and Felicity hums to herself then smiles a bit wildly at her wrist with the bracelet. Once someone gave her a plaited hair bracelet, but she can't see someone's face, only a smudge… a dream of it.

Rachel eyes her. 'Gee, Felic…don't you go spare on me.' She knows all too well how Felicity can drift off for a while. There was stuff galore to see and the boys would wait. Mrs C called this 'Respecting the Likes of Others.'… Which most times was okay with her. So she shunts Felicity towards the door, guides her through, catches up one pale hand and leads her to a bench vacated by a veiled woman with a bunch of kids.

Fingering the new bracelet, Felicity continues to see what she saw. Someone who wore off-white cheesecloth shirts, in loose trousers too big for him. It was a good time, she thinks, but a tiny door of doubt has only to open a crack and, giddy, she'll slam it shut. She remembers spidery ferns in brass pots, the tinkle of brass bells, a window hung with a magenta curtain on a verandah with rag rugs…each room permeated by a cloying sweetness. Sickeningly sweet which he purred was bliss. Haywire talk of a third eye which occupied him but refused to exist for her. She blinks; hadn't he told her to wear that bracelet always? So where has always gone?

Several hours have gone. In precise terms, five. But in the mall's lollypop lights of commerce, doesn't light stream on eternally? Night never falls here, and if the realisation fills them with awe, their senses resist. None of the four wants to imagine such a thing... they sense a sort of exasperation, though are powerless to express how they're better sustained by their routines of Edmund House.

'Soon time to go,' Jack warbles and in accord the others agree that Jack understands the spaces of time best. Time can addle them, besides they do not want Jack off rinsing his hands again before they reach home. Home? A place to be. Where, should any of them choose, they can inspect corners of themselves, good or bad.

Nearby a clock strikes. Rachel counts and pushes up thumb and two fingers of one hand. 'Three,' she says. 'okay?'

'Yep. Okay.'

On the way to the post office for Mrs C's stamps, they halt at a fish shop, goggle at filleted leatherjackets, Atlantic salmon, gemfish... poor things dragged out of their element, silvery, glistening, packed about in ice. Jack in particular is taken by a huge, glaucous-eyed snapper, its gullet propped open on a lemon.

Through the plate glass window Felicity shudders at oysters, to point from prawns to mud-pink tuna. A tremor in her hand, she would like to thrust her fingers into the grainy flesh. Sniff the smell of it she can't smell.

'That's a flathead,' Guy states.

'You're a flathead,' and they grin. Guy too, basking in their approval. It's okay to make fun of themselves.

'Chips is not fish,' Guy likes the role of comedian. Sometimes.

There's a queue at the post office. It snakes between piled reams of paper – which Rachel reads to be A4 – fixtures stacked with envelopes, cards, toys and more. In a showcase, mobiles for sale set Jack worrying how to make a call, not that he worries to whom.

The wait seems interminable. They consult about going to the top of the line; after all they only want a book of stamps, just one for Mrs C, until Felicity states that will upset someone, maybe trigger trouble.

'I'll go,' sensing a purpose, Rachel offers; after all isn't she the one with Mrs C's $5 tucked away in her purse? No, out of character, Felicity is firm, very firm. They must stick together. No matter what. So they shuffle towards the front of the post office queue, people at their separate work stations on the long counter; among them a girl, pretty, but for a rash of pimples, another with an Eastern tinge to her looks like Rachel, a lithe Indian male and a smiley fellow with red hair and a booming voice with his: 'Next please…'

Four abreast their turn will come. Rounded shoulders, chin tucked to throat, Guy reaches down to scratch a calloused heel; bumps the man ahead, smart in a navy business suit.

A frog stare from an overheated face fixes on Jack, slides down to Guy, lifts to Felicity, Rachel watchful for whatever may or not happen. 'So the circus has come to town' is bitten out between sharp teeth. 'Idiots.'

Guy, clumsy in his many-angled world, reels up, a display of gift-sized boxes tottering as he begins to gibber then hoot. Not to be outdone Rachel leers, crosses her eyes, lets her mouth sag cretin-like. A helpless something – rat-a-tat – comes over Felicity's face… then banishing it her mood switches.

'You need a good cuff on the ear. Cause, take my word for it, we're more near to sane than you,' she pipes with aplomb. What's more she has something else to add. 'We're unique and mysterious too.'

'A mob of orangutans.' He turns to bystanders. 'They belong in a zoo…' and an interjector paces forward, mouth set, ready with his retort. Next, leaning forward from her place in the queue, a blonde teenager's expression is frozen in disgust and she raises the bottle of mineral water clenched in one hand.

Though not before there's a flurry of booklets, rubber stamps, pencils, pens. Physically adroit, graceful as a gazelle the young Indian leaps the dividing counter. He clutches the lapels of the business suit over the man's throat.

There's the strangulated question: 'You got a weakness for strays?'

'Yes, sir, I have.' He pitches to follow with a snorting laugh and his perfect teeth gleam like white jewels. 'Not only have I been a stray myself, sir,' disdainful, he's polite, 'but I've had to deal with curs like you.' Someone cheers, someone claps. 'So if the roadshow is over, sir,' he slicks black hair, 'please make your apologies then take your business to the counter.'

'What!'

'Make your apologies. Sir.'

'You're mad as a rattlesnake. No, a bloody cobra.' The dispiriting smell of bigotry wafts with the starched smell of stationery. 'And a bloody BLACK cobra at that.' He jabs the air. 'BLACK as pitch.'

'Next please.'

Mrs C's book of stamps in Rachel's purse, her voice is high. 'Where's Jack? Oooh, nooo!' But Jack has not taken himself further than the door. 'Phew.'

'Let's go,' Guy's tongue courses from one corner of his mouth to the other and he's patting pockets for his bus pass, the shiver in his blood quietened. Soon there'll be little more than hazy recall. Yet if Guy is poised to leap forwards, Jack is not. His face a blank mask, he refuses to budge from the post office step.

'Get up Jack'… but Jack doesn't respond… it's as if a gap has opened; the others lost to him. Did Felicity intuit such an eventuality? Stick-limbed she seats herself down beside him on the concrete under an aluminium awning, wordless to search for, and ease, whatever clamours in his head.

'Jack, you smell like a horse,' Rachel whispers in his ear. She's told him this before and it cheered him lots. Cheered her too, and she sniffs the lovely pungent smell of horses – steamy droppings, gluey grass – and dusty air from way back when the sun poured through trees like ginger smoke or gold.

Jack's owl eyes could be blinking in further distress when Guy squats down, one big knee to rub Jack's. 'Give us a bit of your barley sugar,' Guy cajoles, sort of croons the words. 'Mine's eaten up,' he wriggles closer, and if sobs well in Jack's chest soon, like a miracle, he's batting the small space between them, getting up, dragging back from somewhere, digging in his pocket and order – his order – is refilling his head.

'Time to go, get the bus,' and if uncertain what's real, what's not in this merry-go-round of a place, Jack re-establishes the direct link, and forgetting his anguish – if that's what is was – he moves ahead to the exit and out.

'Wait for me…'

There's still loaded sunlight sharp as lemons and now a warm wind. Traffic snarls, sorts itself out. Crossing onto the footpath a mutt of a dog, ears pricked and smelling like an old carpet, appears from nowhere. No apparent owner, close, it lopes at Jack's heels. Protectively?

'Well bugger me,' says an aged bowler in his white gear, *à propos* of nothing in particular in the bus shelter, and a girl whose eyes were glued to a comic raises them to skitter sideways to the man. A woman extends fleshy, dough-like ankles as she waits on the slatted bench, bends to examines them and heaves a sigh.

No one examines the Edmunds. No pitying or disapproving glances their way; no clicking sounds from the sides of censuring mouths. The 509 duly arrives. 'Put that out, sonny', orders the driver to a youth on the first of the steps. 'Sonny' with bad skin, a concave chest, 'that' a cigarette drooping an inch of ash between Sonny's lips.

'Awgh!' He drags the word out.

'Don't you ever learn? No smoking.' He snorts. 'You want to wheeze your life away through rotten lungs?'

Rachel, on the smoker's heels, registers interest. 'What colour's rotten lungs?' and is disappointed to be told: 'Black.'

Jack behind her is forlorn, slack-jawed, rubs his eyes. Where's the driver who drove them here? This fellow wears a cap perched on a cabbage-round head. And yawns. The earlier driver called him 'mate', while this one shows no sign of having met him before. Sucking his teeth, he slides into the seat by Rachel; the back seat which holds four being already occupied seems to prompt an obscure displeasure in him: 'Stick together' winnowing through his mind?

Passengers in, the door hisses to close. Engine running, gears engaged. Rachel's eyes are on the passing street: pedestrians, delivery vans, an outdoor coffee shop... She presses her nose to the glass while Jack begins to twitch then mouth unspoken words. His upper lip damp, there's a tang like nettles in his nose. The air feels bruised. His forehead hurts, not as if bumped, but hurts with stabs like pins. There's noise too, but more of a hum. What to do? Knees braced forwards, he bangs his forehead on the seat in front where someone's wearing a straw hat with a raffia bow. Again. And this hat starts to revolve, circles towards him.

'What the...?' In a flicker of impatience an eyebrow is cocked. Then: 'You all right?'

'Course he's all right,' Rachel's voice is steady, sure, though she's faced away from Jack. 'And we got rights', bemused she sing-songs as she lolls with the movement of the bus. 'Gee, Jack,' a wistfulness creeps through in a stringy remembrance. 'Look at that beau-uuti-ful cow, ' and the bus slows alongside a billboard advertising dairy products... fresh milk, cream.

As suddenly as he needed to bang his forehead, the need fades. Hands loose in his lap, sunk in himself he's silent, vague with the flux and flow of his inner sights. His expression almost of repose, whatever is happening in his orbit is disconnected from him. Arrived at their bus stop, Jack cannot think exactly how to stand up, while – first out – Felicity gawkily presses one foot on the instep of the other as she waits. And hears a pair of birds squawk on a power line above. Or do they grizzle?

Fatly thrumming his thighs, still aboard the 509, and seated furthest back where he'd tried to count all the stops, Guy won't give way to allow someone pushing at his rear to hurry him. Not till Jack is off and safe... and is ready to punch anyone who tries that on, ready too with: 'Don't mess with us.'

Exhaust from a veteran truck floats by, any salty whiff from the sea unnoticeable; long gone, distanced by housing, parking lots.

On the uneven pavement a toddler on a trike trundles after a big brother who, over a shoulder, flings back: 'Get a move on, stupid.'

Stupid! Guy bunches fists and a nerve jumps in one eye. Stupid! And he runs ahead of Jack, Rachel and Felicity in order to overtake the little kid's minder. Rasping from heat and exertion he places himself in his path. 'Stupid!' Forehead sweaty, patches between his shoulder blades, under his armpits too. 'Why you calling him Stupid?'

The astonished boy turns surly. 'What's it to you?' He glares, turns away and the toddler catches them up, his fingers little piglets on the handlebars of the trike, compact cheeks flushed, his soft-boiled eyes on Guy.

'You just mind who you call that…' and 'STUPID' slaps out of him from a tunnel of tightening air, squeezes like a vice. His vision fogs up. Clears… and he sees… no, he swallows in jerks, doesn't want to look… big people. Not fat – like him – but BIG. Grown people; mismatched men and women with their eyes full of scorn, their hands clenched on shapes that hurt: sticks, rulers, stubby whips who sent him to dark rooms with hairy curtains, and his mouth could have been filled with stones. Next… muddled in time… slapping hard at his own face, Guy rehearses yet again, for what he could never do, nor wish to do.

'Piss off.'

'Pith off,' imitatively issues from the rosebud of the small, wet mouth.

An aggressive whine… then backwards in retreat from the kid and his brother, stumbling, Guy is also in retreat from… What? Jigsaw puzzles. Where the key pieces have gone missing, yet doesn't he breathe what were once customary smells? Misery and wet pants in a place of cabbage, damp, mould… and pursing lips, he wants to spit. Spit out the stones.

'Guy?'

Hands up, covering his ears against angry shouts… then… 'Guy…' he's hearing… 'Guy…' carolling from Felicity and Rachel and the shouts subside.

'Yep,' and they're skipping him along between them. Improvising a sort of dance and head spinning a bit he's returned from gloom to what has become his recognisable world with both belief and trust. Where nobody cuffs his ears, hits out at him, bruises him black and blue… and the numbing loss in him lessens.

'Guy?"

'Yep,' tone lightened, he sheds his scowl. Jack to their right, girded on either side by Felicity and Rachel, he opens his mouth, laughs. Something gone wrong is okay… and if he knows what's happening, no matter he hasn't the words to tell. Pain blunted, phantoms banished… What will there be for tea?

Late afternoon, now under a sky strung with elongated coppery clouds, birds twitter, caw. What's more – whoopee – aren't they in sight of home: Edmund House? His pulse jumps. With joy. Familiar sounds, familiar smells… where everything stays the same.

~ ~ ~

At the worn threshold Rachel fishes for her key to the unlocked door, repeats the ritual at the door of the room she shares with Felicity. Shakes the knob. While there are no locks on Edmund House's interior rooms she considers it's a responsible thing to do. What Mrs C calls: 'setting a good example'.

'Suppose you forgot your key today?' she questions Felicity as invariably she does with a hint of conceit, never expecting an answer, never feeling ill-used. Felicity's gaze settling in the space between them, she is flushed with the good feeling, as always, that Felicity relies on her.

Briskiness overtaking him, Guy heads to the kitchen. Not for food but to help. Hasn't Mrs C allotted him this special job; allowed him to shape the square butter pats, arrange them on plates... one for each table. They'll be expecting him; cook and the girls in aprons tied at the back. Likely they'll tell what's for tea: chops, sausages, maybe a roast, stewed fruit or jelly, ice cream, bread and butter with jam if you want. He likes apricot best. What's more, it's him they ask to twist the caps off the big jars. Lever up the lid from the *Golden Syrup* tin.

'G'day, Guy.' And 'G'day,' he responds, routinely pleased to be here among the pots and pans, workbenches and the big stove. Yes, he must not lick his fingers once he starts, and yes, he must wash his hands at one of the steel sinks, dry them on a paper towel.

'Wash your hands first,' he mutters, half-sings in a low voice and as the water sluices from the tap, he supposes that Jack's time in Jack's head has sent Jack off to do the same.

Six o'clock and Mrs Carmody rings the outsized brass bell kept alongside an elaborate old plant stand. Oddly important because long ago they belonged to somebody else, they're two of the few surviving pieces from the original contents of Edmund House, apart from a vast useless sideboard in the out-of-bounds garage, the attic flat over it. Glum but patient at her side, Jeff, the boy who reads the clouds, can be a worry; unable to hide his dejection each evening when dark comes down... as if the day only fails for him. It's proven a useless exercise attempting to interest him in the stars. The large picture book 'Know Your Stars' she's given him, hoping he'd enjoy the illustrations, has never been opened and she's planning to find time to sit with him to explore it together. Maybe next week.

Smiling at her charges – the majority banging or clattering over the meal – she chooses to let them settle then eat, before she joins them to hear the business of their day.

'Mrs C, Mrs C...' stocky Kate with her cherubic face, pretty curls, spongy upper arms, raises a band-aided thumb. It's Mrs C who zips up her jacket when she's cold.

'What is it, Kate?' She reminds herself to check Kate's file; her fortieth birthday due and a party to arrange. This is easy for Kate: balloons, plenty of whistles and she'll be ecstatic to add another Barbie to her collection.

'I were wery, wery brave,' Kate lisps, takes seconds to think. 'When it was hurted, you know.' Wrists flapping, fingers spread, she circles both hands. Her pantomime.

'Good girl. Well done.' Her expression is solicitous. 'Good girl,' she repeats. 'It'll be better soon.' and feels herself smile when she takes a tangled ribbon from Kate's pocket, spools it over her own fingers and loosens it to spool bandeau-like round Kate's forehead, thankful Kate doesn't demand further attention. Another mental note: inspect her cloud-boy, Jeff whose wrist she's bandaged because he won't leave the scab there to heal.

Glancing up from lowered lashes Felicity brushes by her to weave her path to join Rachel, who sits straight-shouldered, preening in what must be her new tank top, her mouth a startling purple bow. Arching an amused eyebrow, Mrs Carmody's hands tighten. Felicity somehow smells of childish things, the best of childish things: sugary kisses, sandcastles, baby soap, clean hair... Again she refuses to let her imagination overheat. Privilege and uncompromising parents had in no way prepared the young Felicity for real life; shown by example, or any means, how to shape a sense of self. A breakdown, hospitalisation, a male psychiatric nurse; rules were broken, a weakness breached. His charm, on show enough to the little rich girl he proceeded to rob, was reptilian... a fevered depiction of greed and chance. Run to ground in a hippie hideout, the parents wreaking revenge triggered a sense of loss... tipped the balance.

Mentally she raps her knuckles. With all she encounters as an employee of the Department, she tries to keep a moderate and centred view. A balance of perspectives... over-involvement carries risks. There have been times when she's wanted to plunge into apology – shout – not only at individuals but at a society that ignores and abuses the helpless who are unable to conform to the norm. Yet restraint wins the day. Aren't there public-spirited projects, unsung individuals, volunteers, committed professionals, fundraisers, benefactors? Her mind balloons, and she pouts. Plus the inevitable paperwork!

'Hi, Mrs C' Grinning, Guy rocks into view.

'Hi, Guy,' who brings with him a mingled whiff of treacly hair oil and kitchen. 'Did you have a good day?'

'Sure did, sure did.'

'Good. You can tell me about it later,' and as she begins to count her flock she hopes they remembered the book of stamps. Four, six, ten, eleven... Her brow buckles, she re-counts. Again. Her teeth nibble her lip. Eleven! Who's not here? Missing! Her mind sharpens; in moments she determines... Jack! Essential not to startle her charges. She won't question any of them regarding Jack's whereabouts – where last seen – before she makes a thorough search. Deliberate, focused, the communal rooms first – could Jack be myopically watching television? Next the recreation room with ping-pong table, carpet bowls, the bathrooms. No. Shoulders stiffening, she frowns. After a quick search of the bedroom he shares with Guy, she dodges in and out of each of the others, crouching low, a crick in her back, to peer under beds – some messy, unmade – extracts the odd sock, papers, a pair of tights.

Grave, she rolls her eyes. Unlikely, but with uneasy annoyance she thinks of her own rooms as well as the office, laundry, tool room, kitchen…

'Any of the kids here?' Customary, if not strictly correct, that the residents collectively are 'kids', for the present she chooses to with-hold his name. Past the storeroom, the pantry, pushing through fly-screen doors, the dishwasher hums. Apple snow and custard are being ladled out for dessert and in this light the new kitchen hand with the port-wine birthmark which covers most of her neck can appear to have sustained an attack.

'Nope,' and somebody hunkers down by the big table, halloos: 'Cum out, cum out wherever ya are…' while somebody bangs a saucepan, somebody laughs like a high quacking duck.

Where else? Broom cupboards with the smell of overused air, linen cupboards, cupboards under the stairs. Not yet quite un-nerved but, knuckles to both cheeks, she's tense to say the least. How long before she must contact the police: lift the phone, thread this dread through the wire to the local station.

Out of earshot: 'Jack,' she forces herself not to shout, 'Jack… answer me if you hear me. Please.' Giddy, not for the first time, it occurs to her that after its long occupation Edmund House might harbour ghosts. She shivers; with a secret life of their own. She paus-es, blinks… A framed window and all she sees is her faint reflection against the gathering night, guesses her expression is pinched. She runs a finger over one eyebrow, then the other. With never more than a passing interest in fashion, presumes she's seen as frumpy. And shaking her head, grimaces; wonders if she's imagining an accelerated clock racing to midnight.

'Mrs C! Are you losing it? Cracking up, nuts?' She's chastising herself, she could be labelled blindingly immature. Her instinctive response has to be 'NO.'

Of late she's caught herself feeling curious that if she were a woman more concerned with appearance, aging, wouldn't she be aware of the delicate skin around her eyes? Rub it and her neck with cream before bed? A dear friend with whom she's worked, accommodates to her advancing years and the vicissitudes of life by talking to a whiskey glass. Mrs Carmody shrugs. She was warned that this job required a robust identity, flexibility... but, apart from a few hiccups, a little hesitation, she's been willing to stretch herself. She smiles, her lips a sealed line. Off duty she never refuses a drink. Would only in a grave circumstance cancel her weekly massage... tail bone right up to the back of her neck.

There's still her office, bedroom and private sitting room... her hand on the bannister skims the wood, to sense the tentacles of time that must have encompassed all the lives that have been lived here. How many hands must have run up and down it? She halts at the bend of the staircase: whose? Hard questions.

Office, bedroom, bathroom, in her sitting room she pauses. Exhausted, flops into the easy chair plump with cretonne cushions beside her desk with its stacks of paperwork to be dealt with. Is she over-reacting? Bordering on the dreaded burn-out? Hardened? Or worse, disconnected, her brain in an early stage of atrophy? She leans her head back, closes her eyes. Will take a break; maybe ten minutes. Take stock. Do her best to conjure up an escapist trick in her mind. With the many futilities of the past years she's no self-appointed arbiter. Didn't she abandon judgements after a stinging adolescence, followed by a youthful marriage where her every defect was made abundantly clear?

Tony Carmodos... neither honest nor dependable, absorbed with his own needs, never hers – still with a trace of foreignness to his voice, and a cranky stomach, had his own take on brutality. Yes, brutality. How had he arrived in her life? She presses fingers hard to her skull.

Mouth ugly, with just four words weighted by two questions he presented her with the choice: 'You going or staying?' A sort of giggle rises in her throat. If she'd tried to think along with him it wasn't for long; had packed that night. One suitcase and a shoulder bag.

Pieces of the puzzle have gone missing and she's thankful. Vague why she married him, she's crystal clear why she divorced. And with what followed – the right man for the right moment – to find the right ongoing man was not a priority. No longer hostile, she's shaken off memories, come to hold few grudges against life, little abiding bitterness.

How uncomplicated in contrast to her 'kids' here. Trauma can happen anywhere; ineradicable for hundreds of reasons. Didn't the numbers of proven child abuse and neglect rise 20% last year? Nationally notifications are also on the rise. She snorts. Substantiated cases of damage from infancy upwards, kicked off by Fate? Blighted genetics, drugs, random couplings, medical errors, poverty – whatever – all often associated with obscene emotional and physical abuse. When loving care was withheld. Too many 'Records' documented as: 'Collateral Damage.'

But turmoil impedes further thoughts... and she fumbles to reach the box of tissues on the desk. Where she'd all but forgotten in its lower drawer she has – secreted an ink-blurred copy she made at the State Library archives from a newspaper report of 1945... Sept 10 1945. Why now? Why, as from time to time over her years here, is she again stung by the injustices most of her charges suffered prior to the shelter found at Edmund House? Pervasive human and social issues still under-regarded; altruism, kindness seen as an abstraction, airy-fairy. Not for your average citizen. Who can radiate intolerance.

Like a second voice in her head she recalls what prompted Henry Wansell Edmund – in perpetuity – to set up a legal framework to establish care for twelve needy individuals. Stunted by nature, or limited by their circumstances, they were to be afforded physical safety and protection, thanks to his generosity

Which she knows. Indeed, knew before she accepted this position... curiosity leading her to research and that research revealing. It seems subconsciously she's kept details; can still feel a charge bang through her heart, go squeamish at thoughts of what events lay before and beyond the year 1945.

TRAGIC DEATH OF INFANT SON OF PROMINENT FAMILY

At the inquest held by the Magistrate, Mr Arthur J Blayney of the Coroner's Court, into the tragic demise of two-year old Henry Wansell Edmund jnr. only child – and heir – of landowner and businessman Henry Wansell Edmund and his wife Dulcie Janet Edmund (née Robertson), Mr. Blayney expressed that in his view Mrs Edmund had exhibited extreme careless neglect of a son in good physical constitution but parlous mental health. This was attested to by friends and employees who had observed the family and were aware of the circumstances.

Further investigations are under way.

How to disentangle truth from rumour? But, following this public statement the popular press of the time had made a meal of the case: purple prose plus horrific suggestion. Dulcie vacuous, vain, shrill,16 years her husband's junior. An insular upbringing, reading matter confined to light – very light – romance and fashion magazines, silly flirtations. Absorbed with her hair, figure, money and the social standing this afforded, slyly she was quoted as having said – true or false – that she was 'never keen for kiddies but a pretty little girl could have been all right'.

In contrast, reportage on Henry was kindness itself. A man of integrity. Woolly brown hair and a battalion of teeth bravely on show in public, known to be scrupulous in business dealings. A victim of heightened parental expectations, in adversity he was a man of inner strengths. Loved his sad little son… what's more… developed an inner fortress against family secrets. Destiny.

Mrs Carmody chews at the skin of her inner cheek. Secrets? Destiny? Everyone, every family, has something. 'Normal' a slippery concept; but the late Dulcie and Henry Edmund are not some past jigsaw she would attempt to piece together today.

However, what's incontrovertible is that at a date of his choosing, having anchored all legalities, finances, tied each knot to his satisfaction and brought to fruition a rare investment in damaged lives, Henry sat down to a final dinner with a group of trusted friends at Edmund House. Favourite dishes, accompanying wines: Roquefort, Peach Melba and cream followed the veal. At length, after farewelling his guests, with a final brandy – Courvoisier Napoleon – he settled down for the night. Died.

~ ~ ~

God! The time? Her watch tells her it's late. Gritting teeth she pulls in her stomach, stands, reaches for the royal blue cardigan with matching royal blue skirt. Her Mrs C outfit. Uniform.

Her feet in the orthopaedic shoes take wings. Anxiety turns to anger. Where the hell is Jack? She can no longer postpone questioning Rachel, Felicity, Guy and the rest. Calm, she must be calm, though she'll need the discipline of a monk if she's to remain so. Resolute, she pushes her glasses hard to the bridge of her nose. Panic can seize any of them, infect the others, chaos ensue. A dry sob rises in her throat. Isn't each and every one of them lost in some way? Dear God, no mordant reflections. Pity discolours your judgement. Going down that path helps no-one.

Jack? Faced with blank stares, rolling eyes, nods or indifference from his co-residents, Mrs Carmody emphasises that she means THIS afternoon after someone excited shouts yes, when they were at the zoo. Which was a month ago, recalls a funny incident… a monkey snatching someone's banana.

Today, she wants to prompt. Does; widening her eyes. 'Today?' No useful response. She manages to cut short what could be a lengthy version of a movie starring Kylie Minogue. Noise goes on, her heart-rate goes up. Not good.

'Felicity?' And Felicity interweaves her fingers, knots her hands, and if something stirs in her expression, her eyes are glued to her new bracelet.

'Rachel?' And Rachel alarmed is mollified, out of who-knows-where to call up early skills… twitch nostrils at riverbank smells. 'He's rounded up in the home paddock with the new mob. Safe. Real safe.'

'Guy?' And Guy, licking up the last of the custard, lifts a moist gaze to hers, belches into a wrist. He stands, the plate falls, cracks. Then straining up on his toes, clown-like he capers about, ready to lumber past her. Determined, but firm, she pulls at his arm. 'Guy?'

In what she recognises as a distracted tone: 'Find Jack, find Jack, find...' he begins to babble and, with presence of mind she holds tight, restrains him while she directs the rest – again firm – to finish up, stack their plates. Go off to their customary evening routines. Max and Jennie – the night staff – are due and she'll thankfully enlist them in the search.

'Find Jack, find Jack, find...'

'Yes, we'll find Jack,' she humours him, spreads her palms, 'so off you go PLEASE, with the rest.' Instead Guy gives a sort of quack, disentangles his arm from hers and at a fast waddle makes for the front door. 'Guy, where are you going?'

'Musta left Jack at the bus stop,' he's sweating already as he turns to her with satisfaction. 'The 509.'

'I don't think so.'

'Yep, yep...' and it strikes her that Jack could have strayed beyond the house, the garden. But not as far as the area fronting the Council building with its boxed shrubs where three benches are cemented into a wider footpath. Taking Guy with her is a liability but there's not the time to settle him down. Yes, they'll skirt the immediate neighbourhood, ten minutes, then if not... the police.

Plumply running, she hears him grunt with effort before drifting to a stop to scout up and down the street at intervals, searching. Guy raises his eyes to the night sky. Within sight of the bus stop he props, cocks his head to consider Mrs C still attached to him; she doubly anxious not to lose him too.

'We must get back, Guy,' she states having encountered a lone man walking a dog; established he's seen no-one but them since he left his front gate.

'Where?'

'Where?' Speculative, she peers up to Guy .

'Where to get back.'

'Home,' she says, feels him vibrate, then relax, almost – and she's fanciful – as if he's transmogrified to Alice and home is Wonderland.

Nearly dark but not quite, on arrival a relieved Max flings open the front door shadowed by the steeple-high magnolia grande flora. Max who just last week, with a certain profundity said of Guy: 'Big fella with his goofy grins doesn't steer the same as us.'

The night air was now regulated by a bit of a breeze after the earlier heat. 'Okay?' he queries, but before Mrs Carmody can fill him in, half-excited-half-frightened, wilful, Guy refuses to come indoors, turns on his heel.

'Find Jack, find Jack,' he's shouting, fixed and staring at the outer building overgrown by creepers, the inky outline of the attic flat above.

Quick to suppress: 'he won't be there', she rasps out at Max to fetch a torch, follow her, yanks her skirt thigh-high, runs. Yet somehow made nimble by the action Guy reaches the barred door ahead of her. His hands boxer fists, he lurches from foot to foot then charges, he won't be kept out.

'Guy! Stop!' This instruction louder than she intended, she's afraid he'll thrash about, injure himself, bring what could be the rotten lintel down. 'Stop!' again… prays her voice holds authority, but this is lost in the crash of splintering wood. Lost also is her vision of the scene, the light crepuscular, a murky black before Max arrows light from a heavy torch, a slim Maglite in his other hand.

'Stand back,' he orders her. 'Stand back: this place is only held together by them vines. Crikey, where's the boy?' and in frantic circles he pierces the gloom for the 'boy'... middle-aged Guy. Then: 'Christ,' he spits between clenched teeth. 'Big Boy wouldn't be crazy enough to put a foot on them stairs!'

'What do you mean?' Mrs Carmody whispers, knowing what he means. Fallen into disrepair, unsafe; vines snaking through cracks and a broken window, she recalls how she came across a report on this same outbuilding more than eighteen months ago when minor work was underway re-paving the entrance to the main house. That report pre-dated three years! Funds for restoration had been swallowed up elsewhere, demolition mooted but never carried out.

Guy! Where is he? The air rancid, revolting with something dead... a bird, a cat... and who knows what other detritus accumulated over time. A flattening silence ringing in her ears is punctuated by the squeals of rats. Her nerve endings crimp with disgust.

'GUY, GUY...' his name bounces in the dismal light. He must be frozen in fear and this same flattening silence she hears. Again the rats, then the sound of him puffing. God, is he levering up from where he's fallen? 'GUY!'

'Yep, Mrs C...' and dim as it is now sees his outline as he makes to put a foot, then another on the laddered stairs. Crash; the second step collapses under his weight.

'Grab this,' Max shoves the torch at her, 'keep it trained on us.' he dashes forward and unsteady, dust particles swimming through the beam she's able to focus on them; Guy, in a pleased blear gaping in her direction.

'Stay where you are,' Max throws back at her, and aware of impending panic, he tries not to shout. 'Stay where you are.'

But unable to sustain restraint she stumbles over lumpy objects to reach a hiccuping Guy. 'You're okay, okay. With Max.' She elaborates, 'me too, Mrs C, I'm here.'

'And Jack...'

'No, I don't think so...'she hears a sharp bark from Max; then sobered by second thoughts, should she take this seriously? 'Tell me, Guy, IS Jack here?'

'Maybe, maybe, maybe...' Guy singsongs, while Max disentangles him from shafts of wood.

'Where?' She shines one of the torches full on his face, he scowls, smears his clamped eyelids with a filthy hand to lift the other high, points upstairs. 'Guy!' she commands, moves a step forward.

'Maybe, maybe,' his tone amplifies her anxiety. She takes the decision that she – small boned and light – must climb up. Take the chance; Guy in all likelihood expecting her to do something heroic as well as mad. She feels, rather than sees what could be an encouraging grin.

Concentrating every muscle as if she's a trapezist on a tightrope and swinging a torch, the sullen air enfolding her is fraught with danger, plus the noxious smells. Legs trembling, she arrives at the top, puts a foot to the sagging floorboards. Visibility is marginal, meagre light from a window and beyond, a rising moon.

Jack! She registers immense relief. Body shuddering, he's on his stomach, a blanket half pulled over his head, toes braced against a large box. No; she kneels beside him, can see this is an ancient cabin trunk... faded labels, remnants of leather straps. High on a peeling wall, un-stringed racquets for bygone tennis are clamped in wooden presses.

'Jack, dear…' sickened she feels for his pulse, before he jerks, pulls back, his owl eyes huge, nostrils flared. 'Jack, dear,' she repeats, gives a shadowed smile, aches to tell the abused child who is still to this day apparent in him that she's no threat. Instead she extends her hand to cover his.

Max's call is urgent: 'Mrs C…'

'Jack's here. Safe and sound.' Though she's uncertain and the air in her lungs seems like glue. Then words seem to fall out of her mouth: 'If you could take Guy to the house and Jennie. 'Then with a longing to hold fast to something firm in this treacherous situation: 'bring back the steel ladder. Might need it should the stairs not hold.'

Marked, she feels, by heartbeats, his mouth crookedly open, Jack is persuaded to progress down in jerks, soundless shock. The descent at last negotiated, they leave behind the tainted air, fouls smells, then cross to the house, her fingers clamped about his thin wrist. Can he begin to understand her relief? Once indoors his lips crease in a tentative smile. Vulnerable, it's apparent he wants her to accompany him. So she stands alongside during the lengthy time he rinses his hands… a ballast of sorts.

'Come and eat, Jack,' husky-voiced she says, the ritual completed to his needs before she pats water on her papery-dry lips. If he doesn't acknowledge Rachel or Felicity as he trails her through the recreation room, she's certain he knows they're there. At the sight of a tray set with the omelette oozing cheese, jelly, ice cream, cocoa in a mug, his mouth twitches. With light hands she presses him down into a chair. 'Go ahead,' she indicates… and he tucks in.

'Jack,' Mrs Carmody is hopeful as she tells him – hopeful that in some way he may comprehend – 'you've been looking the wrong way. Back into your past.' This thought leaves her breathless… Dear God, if only it was as simple as that.

A blank fixity, then Jack directs his gaze to hers; probing, but without dread or dismay; no fishy look. Her authority MUST provide trust. A whistling breath wheezes from his throat… and if she's shuddering for him, abstracted she thinks: is he edging past vile stacks of memories no child should retain? With no language for his experiences, his ribs like knives, Jack survived. His twin succumbed… ten years ago at the age of eight. No attendant good fairies at this double birth, she needs to implore – no, beg – to somehow accept there's a God above, or someone, something. She has to believe that some tragedies can be left behind!

'Jack…' her throat jams with words. Then… elbows pressed to his sides, his long neck stretching forward, Jack lays his ear to her cheek.

What can I tell him? floods her mind. Maternal, she pats his shoulder, while above all a part of her wants to acquire some of his pain. Free him. But exhausted, she feels herself wilt, kneads her back with the knuckles of one hand. 'It's been a busy day, Jack. Time for bed.'

Below the window a cat picks its way along a brick wall. Motorbikes stutter to a stop. Light traffic in the street, a distant hooter bleats. The dark suspends everything. No longer endangered, faltering at every step in his days of overlapping need, Jack falls into sleep. And having crossed to a different place… hears no actual sounds.

Not even Guy, who, pounding upstairs later, making an effort to be quiet, can't. After shading his bedside lamp with a pair of underpants – he doesn't want to disturb Jack – next pulling on fresh blue-and-red checked pyjamas he greets himself in the mirror of the wardrobe. Pleased enough he turns his mouth up then down. Trying not to laugh out loud, gee he'd like to share the joke but instead scrunches lips together to hum a bit before he lowers himself to bed. In a sort of dreamy tension, hands interlaced but loose behind his head, they won't stay there long. And good-oh, he likes what these hands of his do. The smell may not be roses but it's okay with him.

Rachel has told him heaps about the amazing facts of sex: about straddling a girl and jerking up and down till she moans, while Mrs C has given him a simple illustrated text to answer his questions. He sure knows how girls look without their clothes... bits of them different from him. As well as where babies come from, but here he's mistrustful. Such an itzy-witzy place and even new babies are big, have heads that measure more than a tennis ball.

Guy sucks his teeth. Gee, he forgot to clean them and gee, he remembers Jack's new toothbrush. Maybe he should give him a shake, wake him up to yank off the plastic and cardboard, use it? Maybe not... and this prompts recalls of the day. That rotten kid in black jeans and t-shirt who booted Jack's bum! He doesn't care if he jumps off a cliff, smashes into the sea, gets chewed up then spat out by sharks. Sharks? Sea? His eyes float on waves and... he can hardly believe it... there's a mermaid. A mermaid who wears a bikini... golden scales... but don't mermaids just have tails? Confused, he trawls lazy fingers through his hair, smells the oil, which squeezes out of its bottle shaped like a guitar. Mrs C's book about girls has to be wrong. Now the silence has a buzz to it so he whistles tunelessly against it. Again. If something gnaws at him, he heaves over, bed rumbling, and Guy yawns, wandering to find something blank. His mouth opens and he swallows to gulp back: wait for me... He's almost there, but not there. An interval... and he's away.

Close to midnight and in her white cotton nightdress Felicity leans by the window looking down, lingering, towards... What? She's gathered up time unknowingly as if it's air or moonbeams. Languid, she scoops a curtain to each side, then fretful fastens her grip on the windowsill. Because often, when not otherwise occupied – fingers spread – her hands are braced against something that could be rising up at her from below. A waft of melancholy balloons out in a sigh. Now converting to a state of gloomy joy, shadings in her mind are haphazard, begin to coalesce, jell.

She's cradled in arms, hairy arms; and when she turns to the owner of these arms, her nose is tickled by a hirsute chest. She wriggles her toes.

But she wriggles with a real distaste she can't hide, with what seems his favourite game, stiffens in his embrace. His No.1, he says, calls it 'The Grown Up Game'. Here he parts her thighs, pushes about and hurts her which greatly excites him, pleases him.

Then he says: 'Let's be practical'.

'Practical?' She wanted to force herself to turn, force her eyes from what seemed his unfocused eyes. What else to do? Had she, Felicity, maybe invented him? With all the creamy-sweet talk and the possessive words. Who to smile can just bare his teeth.

'Practical?' she was repeating; longing to turn away, from him, muffle dry sobs in the pillow.

'Yep, pale lily of my life. How's about I set up a power of attorney... legal, airtight,' and she's willing enough to give him whatever this is that he wants. Collapsing off her, she's half wondering who he is because his husky voice changes, loses intimacy. More like a brusque shopkeeper listing household items – brooms. Buckets, laundry soaps – to conclude: 'I'll do the worrying – and the spending – for both of us. Yes?' And she's nodding, doesn't speak, doesn't know what to say.

She doesn't know what to say either when he instructs her in 'blow jobs' and at her reluctance, suggests that as a joke she can call them 'turnip tops'. A joke she didn't grasp; yearns to bury this experience.

But playful, he tickles her ears, encircles her neck and she's happy till the pressure increases and she's anxious. Anxious too, when he twists her wrists with what he jeers to be 'Chinese burns'. He can be rough, dreadful, but only once did he burn her with a cigarette, on the wrist, but next day gave her a present in a gold-papered box. This held a plaited hair bracelet, and sort of slippery-eyed, he said she should wear it always. Always? Where has always gone?

Felicity sighs out at the night. Hears the stillness, winces at the burden of half-realised memory. Whose hair made up that bracelet? Whose strands of hair was it plaited from? Not hers; red. Not her mother's; redder... a hot frame round a cross and lemon-lipped face, whose skin was the colour of candle grease.

Time snags and stops. Jumbled up, pin pricks run and jab over her body, and Felicity wants to float off. Somewhere, anywhere. Why was that wide-boned mother forever cross? Smile even at strangers... but leave her out? Was there an emptiness that might have given her a way in? In those pillbox hats and veils, her spiky heels, the bridge-party smiles? A person who was a mother, though she never much wanted to touch her, her little girl? Circle her with the freckled arms she creamed from a white jar on the triple-mirrored dressing table? Arms, which gleamed, smelled nice.

No answers so far, and Felicity hears another question out of time. This she lispingly puts to a man with his back to a harsh light which means he is a blank to her; no eyes, no mouth for her to read. 'Daddy, why doesn't she like me?' And in the semi-dark of the room she shares with Rachel a hot something swells inside her and the heels of her hands jam her ears.

Harder, harder till they ring, but something rings louder – stings – after she's given a hefty cuff. More than a slap, puppet-like, her head jerking to one side. Again.

'How dare you,' the faceless man explodes, then fingers a silk tie. 'It is the duty of every mother – and every parent – to love a child. Don't we give you, Felicity, everything! What's more, my girl, God will punish you if you dare repeat such things.' His words now live on in a reverberating box. 'Outside this house… this house… this house…'

This house! Her breath comes in swift bursts. No matter how hard she tries to examine it, it remains wispy, distant. Instead in the-here-and-now Felicity sets herself to examine the garden below. Speared by moonlight, by night Edmund House's garden is different. Enchanted, Felicity decides, stares down wanting to let this place fill her mind. So… she'll clothe it with a crystal pond where a frog prince lives in disguise. Next, wanded by magic to a glittering coach, but she'll refuse to be handed in by a footman, swept off to the ball. Wasn't gawky Felicity cruelly subjected to ridicule: the worst pupil, her feet dead fish! Never mind; Aladdin's cave shimmers, and from loamy depths a beanstalk climbs heavenwards. Heavenwards? No, she has no intention of setting Jack to climb it, never will. She clutches her arms, pats her bony shoulders… gives herself what could be a hug. Jack belongs here with them and now she'll address herself to blunt the brilliance of the moon. This is what remains.

Distracted by a fitful mutter from Rachel at the end of their room, she folds her nightgown in between her knees and with feline concentration tiptoes back to bed. In days without names tomorrow will come and, seldom given to self-protection, she needs to be asleep. Fast asleep if, in the goblin hours, one of Rachel's nightmares is cranking up, on the way.

~ ~ ~

Educable in certain things and to a given point, Rachel makes no painstaking trek over her life. It's not her way. What she does best alone is drift – she wouldn't know to call it daydream – because Rachel's logic doesn't associate day with dream. Horrid dreams can tumble her into a state of pain. Fear too. Termed 'nightmares' by Edmund House staff, do they have the right to differentiate what happens to her from what happens to them?

'We got rights,' may have become her mantra but: mantra, marsupial, metamorphose… such words mean nothing to her. Sure she makes efforts to be good, feeble efforts if she can't see why she should. Or feels no urge to be good.

Unaware she courted rape – or worse – on arrival from the outback, eager to wear vampish city shorts and skirts, an aging pimp mystified her when, tongue lolling, dribbling, he alluded to her 'eighth wonder of the world'.

'Me what?'

'Yer cunt.' And she'd hooted, doubled up, laughed like a drain.

Today cause and effect aren't lost on Rachel: you spend your money and there's nothing left, you take a shower and you come out clean. Unlike the majority of Edmund House's residents, Rachel got by in what has been explained to her as 'Outside'. If not better, then almost as well as those with more support.

Small-boned, with an Eastern tinge, stark black hair and eyebrows… under what circumstances was she raised in the bush? Jack

– who once drew heart-breaking images in sessions with a psychologist and still has access to paper and paints – often agrees to Rachel's: 'Give us a go.'

Stilt-legged cattle at a waterhole, landlocked emus on the run beside fences which flow to the horizon, bleak rail-heads, quivering echoes conceivably of fettlers' camps... What of the trio of colours she employs? Oranges, reds, mauves... do they signify the earth, a setting sun, lilac-mauve dusks before night comes down?

Yet Rachel leads a double life. She pores over the 'mags'. Women's weeklies, monthlies, quarterlies which find their way to Edmund House are hers when these 'mags' have done the rounds. Skimming page to page, hours are occupied snipping and trimming before, glue poised, she adds to her several scrapbooks. Scrapbooks of brides. Young women floating in diaphanous stuff like fairy floss, smothered in the syrup of nuptials; bridesmaids, tricked up child attendants, flowers, confetti, be-ribboned stretch limos. Humming, genial as a contented top, withdrawn from conversations, tight-knuckled she presses each picture into place, wipes away any excess glue with a cloth. What's more, wherever she can she slices off the appendage that's the groom; makes a little noise, maybe hilarity, maybe satisfaction. Though not before she blocks in strongly marked eyebrows. Black as pitch; like hers. There's one mag she's never wanted to discard. Tattered cover, old, this issue just falls open at page 10, where in detail it records the full splendour of a country wedding .

Among towering gums the homestead fronts a billabong. Spacious rooms are filled with wild flannel flowers, waratahs, kangaroo paw... the verandahs studded by white-painted buckets brimful with bush foliage, plants. Damask sheets covering tables display the mouth-watering spread: pies, triangled sandwiches, cakes, cakes

and more cakes, fondly baked by the local CWA (Country Wom-
ens' Association). Centred stands the wedding cake, top-tiered by a
marzipan bride, groom, two favourite dogs. Recorded too, a pair of
handsome chestnut mares, lovingly groomed, which bore the bridal
couple to and from the church – forever graze in a verdant home
paddock, their happy duty done.

Alone at night, locked in yearning does she fantasise? A wedding where she's the radiant bride? Imagine mists of tulle clasped
in diamonds, shiver in pleasure to the slip of satin as it ripples
down her upheld arms, her body? The here-and-now city air redo-
lent with roses, stephanotis, white lilac? Fluted song from a choir,
flights of doves from a tower? If she does no one knows.

Bedtime and her footsteps resound as she walks over the floorboards but kicking off shoes; no, they're no silver sandals. Definite-
ly not. In duplicitous reality, her left leg thrown over the right then
vice versa, Rachel yanks off work boots, thick socks. Toes scuffed
in the paddocks, or in yards docking tails, drenching. All seasons
– year by year – in the shearing shed helping when permitted, running errands for the shearers' cook. Together with heavy boots for
the men, hers come from the Co-op in town, sturdy, practical, size
7. Don't they cost heaps! One day she believes a pair of jodhpur
boots will be waiting to be collected from the post office: *R.M. Wil-
liams* stamped on the soles, parcelled with a suede *Akubra* with a
chin strap .

Far off in sleep she smells the seasons as they turn: the dry, the
wet; not much that comes between. When she was stick-thin and
didn't wake at night, screaming inside, suffocating. Abandoned
to dust storms where she chokes, floods where she's sucked down,
drowns. Then awake, stretched in fright, tight as a cowhide on
four poles, release is sweet when it dawns on Rachel where she is.
Edmund House. Nose-close, she inspects her hollowed pillow, as-

suring herself it's neither stained nor dingy grey. After which it's safe to get up; no longer inside an awful dream. With its ghostly smells: dead sheep, putrid with lambs or marooned cattle, calves, bloated with gas.

What is blissful is encountering Jack setting off to or from the big bathroom taps. Sometimes she takes his hand, sometimes he takes hers. That's when she goes sort of slack… Makes soft slapping sounds like a lowing longhorn who's dropped her calf… the pull to earth done.

Under a bone-white moon flung high in the sky the night is smooth. Smooth, yielding, as it slants over four of the residents, their worlds closed down; no fat sun to rise out from the east for hours, peer hungrily into their lives.

The distant sea undulates under its eternal rhythm, night birds are quietened in the magnolia grande flora, neighbouring trees. A lone car purrs past Edmund House, night sounds tangle together, evaporate.

Dormant – dead to the world but alive – Guy, Rachel, Jack and Felicity all have something to remember. Nubbles of thought. Wobbly truths. Which, prompted by creases in their brains they may choose – or not – to forget – or maybe to remember.

They have suffered trials, tribulations that could have destroyed them – but have reached their safe harbour, a place to call home. They have their rights – one of which is their span of time in the sun. Who is to say their lives are less precious than any others?

In total twelve residents of Edmund House hoist over in their beds, sprawl, fold foetal-like, thumb to mouth, or repose like statues as they slumber, play games with time. Unravelled from yesterday, going on to to-morrow. Where, when that day opens under a broad sash of blue sky everything will be changed… yet continue on the same.

~   ~   ~

NATALIE SCOTT - A Selection of Reviews

"Powerfully written and formidably intelligent"

Literature Review London

"Writes with a documentary realism and a fierceness that gives uncommon experience urgency"

Sunday Times

"With a style akin to that of Janet Frame, teasing out layers of meaning hidden behind the simple and the conventional. Scott probes the psyche with skill and knows how to touch a nerve gently"

The Age

"Writing is careful, witty and always finely crafted. It has links with Shirley Hazzard's deliberate style but is more in touch with the contemporary and less puritanical"

The Australian Book Review

"Electric vividness with the poet in Miss Scott's make up, attempting to come to terms with the demands of prose"

The Scotsman

"All characters,major and minor, have reality, plus style and grace. For me, the short story remains THE fictional form.Natalie Scott's stories are some of the most stylish currently being written in Australia"

Professor of Australian Literature, University of Sydney

"Natalie Scott's stories capture intensified moments and always manage to expose the rawness of a situation. Her dramatic skills are impressive. She handles sentimentality, themes and issues with a light touch and a selective eye".

Overland

Born and educated in Sydney Australia, Natalie Scott was a freelance writer before her novels, short stories, non-fiction, books for children and audio books were published internationally. A columnist for *The Sydney Morning Herald* and *The Australian*, she also wrote for television and radio and has contributed to many literary magazines, to include *The Griffith Review, Southerly, Westerly* and *Meanjin*.

Her first novel, *Wherever We Step the Land is Mined*, published in Australia, the UK and the USA in 1980, was a penetrating study of a woman coming to terms with surviving on her own.

Her second, *The Glasshouse*, examines with insight and sensitivity the anguish of debilitating old age and the guilt and trauma suffered by those who make selfish choices.

In two volumes of short stories, *Eating Out* and *Eating Out Again*, she created an array of characters from all walks of life, united by the common human need for sustenance. *Eating Out & other stories* (read by the doyenne of Australian theatre, Ruth Cracknell) won the National Library's TDK Audio Book Award for Unabridged Fiction and the Women Writers Biannual Fiction Award. Ruth Cracknell also recorded *The Glasshouse* for ABC.

Wobbly Truths takes the reader into territory alien to most of us, in which the author reveals the inner lives of people on the margins of society, the disabled and their family members, who have suffered life-changing and wobbly events through no fault of their own.

International reviewers have compared her work with Shirley Hazzard (but less puritanical), Janet Frame, the *New Yorker's* Dawn Powell and Nathalie Surat of France. Her many admirers know she is in a class of her own.

News for readers is that she has completed her third novel and a further collection of short stories, to be published in 2022.